WELCOME

Hi everyone! My name is Dee Marley, or as many know me, D. K. Marley, and I am the CEO of The Historical Fiction Company. I am proud and honored to take over Historical Times magazine, and determined to continue the high standards and exceptional quality set by the magazine's founder, Sam Taw. I set out in 2021 at the height of the pandemic to create a haven for historical fiction authors and readers across the world purely out of my own love for historical fiction and my desire to support this amazing community who have taught me so much during my own writing journey.

Now, with the combination of The Historical Fiction Company and Historical Times magazine, along with the new launch of our official podcast, History Bards, it is my hope to continue providing a first-class place dedicated to this special genre that I adore. I look forward to getting to know all of you and as many of you know from visiting HFC, I am available 24/7 and will always answer any questions any of you might have. Here's to bigger and better things for 2023!!

DEE MARLEY
Editor-in-Chief

FOUNDER
SAM TAW

EDITOR-IN-CHIEF
DEE MARLEY

FEATURED SPOTLIGHT
ELIZABETH ST. JOHN

CONTRIBUTORS
ANNE O'BRIEN
STEVE MOYSEY
JULIANE WEBER
D. G. MACDOUGALL
KATERINA DUNNE
GARETH WILLIAMS

SPONSORS
HELENA P. SCHRADER
SUSANNE DUNLAP
TOM DURWOOD
BOOKOUTURE
TESS THOMPSON

CONTACT INFO

1 (912) 577-7407

thehistoricalfictioncompany
@gmail.com

FOR SUBSCRIPTIONS:

www.historicaltimes.org

Subscriptions for
Printed & Online Special
Editions (per issue)
US $19.99 UK 16.06

Annual Subscriptions for
Online Editions (12 issues)
US $35.00 UK 28,12

FEATURED CONTRIBUTORS

ELIZABETH ST. JOHN

Award-winning author of the Lydiard Chronicles and "The Godmother's Secret" - she is a descendant of Elysabeth St. John, sister of Margaret Beaufort, the mother of Henry VII and a member of the Friends of Lydiard Park.

ANNE O'BRIEN

Sunday Times best-selling historical author of "The Queen's Rival", "The Marriage of Fortune", "The Royal Game" and more… selling more than one million copies in the UK and internationally.

STEVEN P. MOYSEY

Moysey's critically acclaimed book "The Road to Balcombe Street" recounts the 1974 IRA siege, and is now a major motion picture releasing in 2023 starring Aml Ameen, Felicity Jones, and Mark Strong.

CONTENTS

ON THE COVER
"Choosing the Red and White Roses in the Temple Garden" by Henry A. Payne (1908–10), pen and watercolour, gouache, gold-leaf and oil. Image by Wikipedia.

6-15 APRIL 1896
FIRST MODERN-DAY OLYMPICS IN ATHENS, GREECE

The 1896 Summer Olympics (officially known as the Games of the I Olympiad romanized: Agónes tis Iis Olympiádas) and commonly known as Athens 1896, was the first international Olympic Games held in modern history. Organised by the International Olympic Committee (IOC), which had been created by French aristocrat Pierre de Coubertin, it was held in Athens, Greece, from 6 to 15 April 1896.

Fourteen nations (according to the IOC, though the number is subject to interpretation) and 241 athletes (all males; this number is also disputed) took part in the games. Participants were all European, or living in Europe, with the exception of the United States team. Over 65% of the competing athletes were Greek. Winners were given a silver medal, while runners-up received a copper medal. Retroactively, the IOC has converted these to gold and silver, and awarded bronze medals to third placed athletes. Ten of the 14 participating nations earned medals. The United States won the most gold medals, 11, while host nation Greece won the most medals overall, 47. The highlight for the Greeks was the marathon victory by their compatriot Spyridon Louis. The most successful competitor was German wrestler and gymnast Carl Schuhmann, who won four events.

On 4 April 1945 the U.S. 89th Infantry Division overran Ohrdruf, a subcamp of Buchenwald.

Buchenwald was partially evacuated by the Germans from 6 to 11 April 1945. In the days before the arrival of the American army, thousands of the prisoners were forced to join the evacuation marches. Thanks in large part to the efforts of Polish engineer (and short-wave radio-amateur, his pre-war callsign was SP2BD) Gwidon Damazyn, an inmate since March 1941, a secret short-wave transmitter and small generator were built and hidden in the prisoners' movie room. On April 8 at noon, Damazyn and Russian prisoner Konstantin

12 APRIL 1945
BUCHENWALD CONCENTRATION CAMP IS LIBERATED

Ivanovich Leonov sent the Morse code message prepared by leaders of the prisoners' underground resistance (supposedly Walter Bartel and Harry Kuhn):

The text was repeated several times in English, German, and Russian. Damazyn sent the English and German transmissions, while Leonov sent the Russian version. Three minutes after the last transmission sent by Damazyn, the headquarters of the U.S. Third Army responded:

According to Teofil Witek, a fellow Polish prisoner who witnessed the transmissions, Damazyn fainted after receiving the message.

As American forces closed in, Gestapo headquarters at Weimar telephoned the camp administration to announce that it was sending explosives to blow up any evidence of the camp, including its inmates. The Gestapo did not know that the administrators had already fled. A prisoner answered the phone and informed headquarters that explosives would not be needed, as the camp had already been blown up, which was not

true. A detachment of troops of the U.S. 9th Armored Infantry Battalion, from the 6th Armored Division, part of the U.S. Third Army, and under the command of Captain Frederic Keffer, arrived at Buchenwald on 11 April 1945 at 3:15 p.m. (now the permanent time of the clock at the entrance gate). The soldiers were given a hero's welcome, with the emaciated survivors finding the strength to toss some liberators into the air in celebration.[36]

Later in the day, elements of the U.S. 83rd Infantry Division overran Langenstein, one of a number of smaller camps comprising the Buchenwald complex. There, the division liberated over 21,000 prisoners,[36] ordered the mayor of Langenstein to send food and water to the camp, and hurried medical supplies forward from the 20th Field Hospital.

Third Army Headquarters sent elements of the 80th Infantry Division to take control of the camp on the morning of Thursday 12 April 1945. Several journalists arrived on the same day, perhaps with the 80th, including Edward R. Murrow, whose radio report of his arrival and reception was broadcast on CBS and became one of his most famous.

12 APRIL 1912
LUXURY LINER TITANIC SINKS IN THE NORTH ATLANTIC

At 11:40 pm (ship's time) on 14 April, lookout Frederick Fleet spotted an iceberg immediately ahead of Titanic and alerted the bridge. First Officer William Murdoch ordered the ship to be steered around the obstacle and the engines to be reversed, but it was too late; the starboard side of Titanic struck the iceberg, creating a series of holes below the waterline. The hull was not punctured by the iceberg, but rather dented such that the hull's seams buckled and separated, allowing water to rush in. Five of the ship's watertight compartments were breached. It soon became clear that the ship was doomed, as she could not survive more than four compartments being flooded. Titanic began sinking bow-first, with water spilling from compartment to compartment as her angle in the water became steeper.

Between 2:10 and 2:15 am, a little over two and a half hours after Titanic struck the iceberg, her rate of sinking suddenly increased as the boat deck dipped underwater, and the sea poured in through open hatches and grates. Almost all of those in the water died of cardiac arrest or other bodily reactions to freezing water, within 15–30 minutes. Only five of them were helped into the lifeboats, though the lifeboats had room for almost 500 more people.

28 APRIL 1789
MUTINY ON THE SHIP BOUNTY

Some 1,300 miles (2,100 km) west of Tahiti, near Tonga, mutiny broke out on 28 April 1789. Despite strong words and threats heard on both sides, the ship was taken bloodlessly and apparently without struggle by any of the loyalists except Bligh himself. Of the 42 men on board aside from Bligh and Christian, 22 joined Fletcher Christian in mutiny, two were passive, and 18 remained loyal to Bligh.

The mutineers finally settled on Pitcairn Island along with several women and chidlren from Tahiti.

14 APRIL 1865
ABRAHAM LINCOLN IS ASSASSINATED

On April 14, 1865, hours before he was assassinated, Lincoln signed legislation establishing the United States Secret Service and, at 10:15 in the evening, Booth entered the back of Lincoln's theater box, crept up from behind, and fired at the back of Lincoln's head, mortally wounding him. Lincoln's guest, Major Henry Rathbone, momentarily grappled with Booth, but Booth stabbed him and escaped. After being attended by Doctor Charles Leale and two other doctors, Lincoln was taken across the street to Petersen House. After remaining in a coma for eight hours, Lincoln died at 7:22 in the morning on April 15. Stanton saluted and said, "Now he belongs to the ages." Lincoln's body was placed in a flag-wrapped coffin, which was loaded into a hearse and es-

corted to the White House by Union soldiers.[318] President Johnson was sworn in later that same day. Two weeks later, Booth, refusing to surrender, was tracked to a farm in Virginia, and was mortally shot by Sergeant Boston Corbett and died on April 26. Secretary of War Stanton had issued orders that Booth be taken alive, so Corbett was initially arrested to be court martialed. After a brief interview, Stanton declared him a patriot and dismissed the charge.

11-17 APRIL 1970
APOLLO 13 LAUNCHES

Apollo 13 (April 11–17, 1970) was the seventh crewed mission in the Apollo space program and the third meant to land on the Moon. The craft was launched from Kennedy Space Center on April 11, 1970, but the lunar landing was aborted after an oxygen tank in the service module (SM) failed two days into the mission. The crew instead looped around the Moon and returned safely to Earth on April 17. The mission was commanded by Jim Lovell, with Jack Swigert as command module (CM) pilot and Fred Haise as Lunar Module (LM) pilot. Swigert was a late replacement for Ken Mattingly, who was grounded after exposure to rubella.

The Apollo 13 mission insignia depicts the Greek god of the Sun, Apollo, with three horses pulling his chariot across the face of the Moon, and the Earth seen in the distance. This is meant to symbolize the Apollo flights bringing the light of knowledge to all people. The mission motto, Ex luna, scientia ("From the Moon, knowledge"), appears. In choosing it, Lovell adapted the motto of his alma mater, the Naval Academy, Ex scientia, tridens ("From knowledge, sea power").

ELIZABETH ST. JOHN

AWARD-WINNING AUTHOR OF "THE GODMOTHER'S SECRET" AND THE LYDIARD CHRONICLES

Elizabeth St.John's critically acclaimed historical fiction novels tell the stories of her ancestors: extraordinary women whose intriguing kinship with England's kings and queens brings an intimately unique perspective to Medieval, Tudor, and Stuart times.

Inspired by family archives and residences from Lydiard Park to the Tower of London, Elizabeth spends much of her time exploring ancestral portraits, diaries, and lost gardens. And encountering the occasional ghost. But that's another story.

Living between California, England, and the past, Elizabeth is the International Ambassador for The Friends of Lydiard Park, an English charity dedicated to conserving and enhancing this beautiful centuries-old country house and park. As a curator for The Lydiard Archives, she is constantly looking for an undiscovered treasure to inspire her next novel.

Elizabeth's books include her trilogy, The Lydiard Chronicles, set in 17th Century England during the Civil War, and her newest release, The Godmother's Secret, which explores the medieval mystery of the missing Princes in the Tower of London.

What literary pilgrimages have you been on in your life?

My novels are inspired by Lydiard Park, the 1,000-year-old country estate that was the seat of the St.John family since the 15th century. Parts of the house date back to that time, and the church of St.Mary, which is within the grounds of the estate, is full of monuments to my ancestors, especially those of the 17th century. When I was writing The Lydiard Chronicles, and The Godmother's Secret, I spent a lot of time at Lydiard, absorbing the atmosphere and knowing that I was walking in the footsteps of my characters.

Tell us the best writing tips you can think of, something that helps you.

Simply showing up every day, even if you don't think you have anything to write. Whether working on a novel, sketching character arcs, or jotting observations in a notebook on a crowded train, being "in the zone" as a writer really helps hone your skill. And reading. Reading widely and in all genres, classics, and the newest releases. Finding a writing buddy or two. Someone who really understands what you're trying to do and can cheer you on or empathise (we need both!).

What's a common trap for aspiring writers, advice for young writers starting out?

Probably trying to write the perfect scene in the very first draft. I think back to writers who were starting out at the same time as me ten years ago, and some of them have yet to complete a work because of editing and re-editing their opening pages. The first draft is just you telling yourself the story. No one will see it, so just start at the beginning and go all the way to the end. There's PLENTY of time for editing (and re-editing, and editing again) later.

How did publishing your first book change your process of writing?

Writing my first book seemed easy – I had been carrying it around inside me for many years. Writing subsequent books was hard work, and I really appreciated and came to enjoy the fine skill of editing.

What was the best money you ever spent as a writer?

Joining the Historical Novel Society, going to their North American conference for the very first time, and meeting the most amazing group of people whom I am still lucky enough to call friends and colleagues. And plucking up the courage to ask Jenny Quinlan if I could send her my manuscript, as we were both leaving for the airport. Four books and four novelettes later, she's still my editor, and I'd be lost without her!

What is an early experience where you learned that language had power?

Writing a story about my cat when I was about eight years old. My teacher, Mrs. Davies, read it out aloud to the class and everyone laughed in all the right places, and clapped at the end.

What's the best way to market your books?

With personal attention to detail, and a consistent commitment. Marketing is a long haul, and I think of it as nourishing relationships – with readers, authors, bloggers, social media followers, and the book community. I spend little or no money on advertising, choosing instead to take a personal approach by doing blog tours, reviews, interacting with social media followers and running promotions. I experiment with both "going wide" and running KDP/ Amazon only, adjusting pricing to meet demand. I also enjoy giving Author Talks at libraries and book clubs, and speaking at conferences.

What kind of research do you do, and how long do you spend researching before beginning a book?

Intense research, because my books are biographical historical fiction, and so the facts are the facts. I can do most of my research online on digital archives and libraries, but I also enjoy field research, where I visit locations and spend time (as I do at Lydiard Park, Bolton Castle and the Tower of London) with my characters.

On average, I spend at least six months researching, before beginning a book, and then commit to daily reading as I'm writing. I then spend a fair amount of time fact-checking with my historical beta readers once the manuscript is ready for review.

What are your ethics of writing about historical figures?

I think it's important to take a fair and balanced view of all historical figures, and so wherever possible I go to source documents or extant materials to understand context and politics of the time. As historical writers, I believe we have to build trust with our readers that we are not only researching and present history accurately, we are portraying historical figures with a clear perspective. Having written about some of the more controversial figures in history – Oliver Cromwell and Richard III for instance – I think it's important to understand them as full characters, not just how history books have depicted them.

Do you read your book reviews? How do you deal with bad or good ones?

I do, because if someone's taken the time to review one of my books, I think it's only right that I should take the time to read it. Of course, we love good reviews, and it's especially rewarding when a reviewer identifies something which really resonates with them. Bad reviews come in different shapes and sizes. If the reviewer had identified a flaw or something they dislike in my writing, I welcome the opportunity to understand and learn. If it's a "troll" who is simply being unpleasant (and sadly this happens all too frequently to all of us) then I turn to my writer group for consolation, a laugh, and put it firmly in the rear-view mirror.

What is the most difficult part of your artistic process?

It actually has changed with each book that I write. Sometimes it's the research, as it was during Covid lockdown, when we couldn't go anywhere, and online resources were scarce. Other times it's the creative part – perhaps it's challenging to find the voice of a main character (particularly historical women who lacked agency) or they simply won't "come alive". When that happens, I turn to my writing buddies with the issue, and between us we usually spark some ideas to get the juices flowing again. Or go for a long walk with my dog. He always listens to me ramble on.

Tell us about your novels or series and why you wrote about these topics.

My historical fiction novels tell the stories of my ancestors: extraordinary women whose intriguing kinship with England's kings and queens brings an intimately unique perspective to Medieval, Tudor, and Stuart times.
I am inspired by family archives and residences from Lydiard Park to the Tower of London, and I've always spent my free time in England exploring ancestral portraits, diaries, ruined castles, ancient churches, and lost gardens. As the International Ambassador for The Friends of Lydiard Park, an English charity dedicated to conserving and enhancing this beautiful centuries-old country house and park, I love to introduce people to my "special place". And as a curator for The Lydiard Archives, a comprehensive digital collection of documents and images about Lydiard Park, I am constantly looking for an undiscovered treasure to inspire my next novel.

What is your favorite line or passage from your own book?

That's hard! I love to world-build and immerse readers in my novels, and I think that's what I'm known for in many instances. But I would say sometimes, there's just a small exchange that can summarize an entire relationship, and this brief encounter between Lady Elysabeth Scrope and her sister, Margaret Beaufort, discussing Henry Tudor's ambition for the throne was a pivot point in The Godmother's Secret. I'm also proud that it's dialogue, for that was the most challenging skill for me to learn!

"You have great ambitions for your son," I say. "At first, you wanted his lands restored, his title secured. Now you dream of the throne for him."
In the darkness of the cloister, Margaret's face is in shadow, but there is no missing the excitement in her voice.
"My son has been named successor to the throne before," she replies. "And these years of exile and separation have been a sacrifice we have both endured, knowing that one day God will guide us back together again. If it is to be, then it will be."
With your guidance. God is but a passenger on your journey. "This is treason, Margaret."
"This is destiny, Elysabeth."

What was your hardest scene to write?

The death scenes are always the hardest for me. Saying goodbye to a character that has inhabited your heart for so long is painful. And when they are my own ancestors, I think I feel an extra pang.

Tell us your favorite quote and how that quote tells us something about you.

"It is never too late to be what you might have been."
George Eliot

I've loved this quote since I was in my twenties, living a very different life, with a demanding career. I resolved one day I would write a book, and thirty years later, I did.

* * * * *

Visit Elizabeth's website at:
www.elizabethstjohn.com

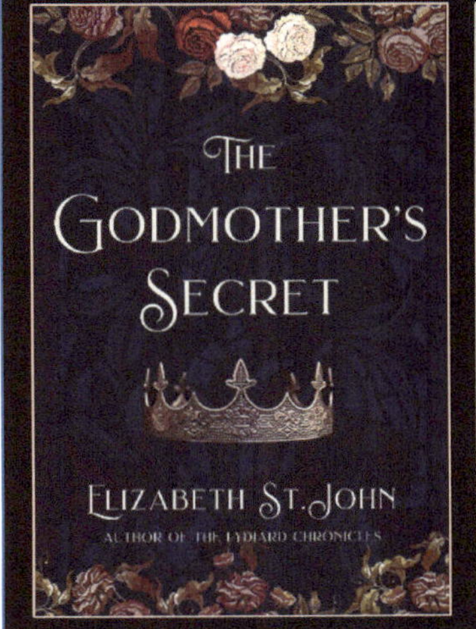

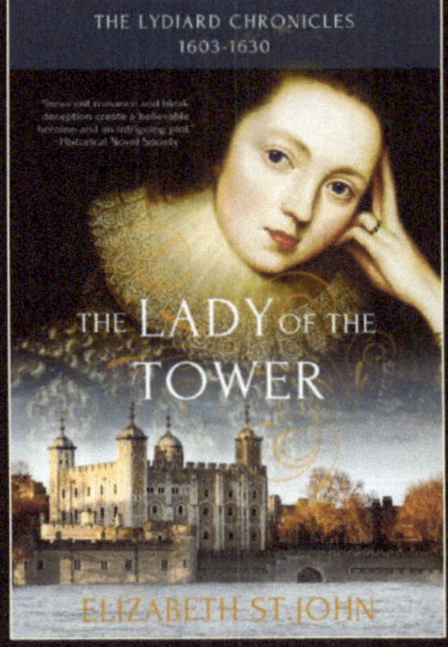

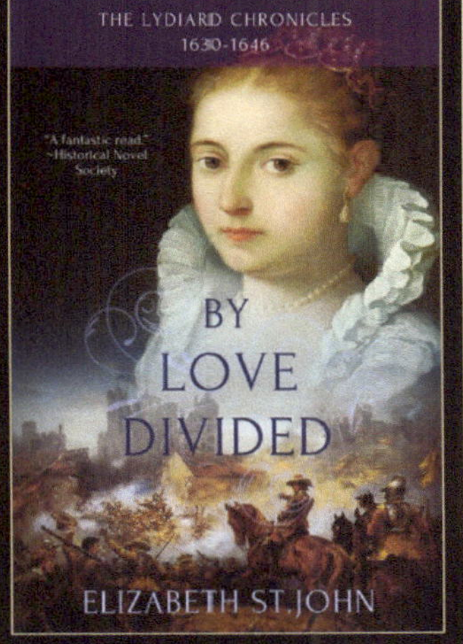

SURVIVAL OF THE FITTEST: What did the Paston Family do in the War of the Roses?

Anne O'Brien

The Paston men who wrote letters are well known useful sources for their comments on what was going on at Court and in the manoeuvring of the powerful magnates in the Wars of the Roses. But what did this middling sort of people actually do when faced with the tragedy of civil war? For many it was a matter of keeping their heads down, to emerge at the end in one piece. If they were unfortunate, their manors would become part of the battleground, fought across and laid waste. If luck was with them, the fighting would pass them by. Whatever happened in the battles, it was good policy to do all they could to keep in the King's good books, or under the beneficial eye of the local magnate. Survival was everything.

The Paston family found it very difficult to achieve either of these two options. To their benefit, their manors, mostly in Norfolk and Suffolk, were never in the path of marauding armies. But attracting the good offices of King or magnate was another matter altogether. The Paston menfolk certainly petitioned Edward IV for the security of Caister Castle and protection for the Paston manors from men such as the Dukes of Suffolk and Norfolk, with recompense for past attacks, but their success was limited. King Edward was not prepared to push for recompense when the support of the Dukes was far more important to him than that of Sir John II Paston.

As for the Dukes of Norfolk and Suffolk, in their relationship with the Pastons they were a law unto themselves. With a weak King such as Henry VI and a troubled King Edward IV with his own difficulties when facing the demands of Warwick and Clarence, the local magnates were given the freedom to follow their own interests. The Pastons became pawns in the local power games. No one was prepared to stop the Duke of Norfolk from taking possession of Caister Castle, the jewel in the Paston crown. John III Paston might hold out in a short siege but the outcome was inevitable. The Pastons lost their castle.   Getting it back would need a miracle.

In the fighting. John I Paston managed to keep out of any battles, focusing on disputes in the courts of law. His sons were not so fortunate. John II and John III found themselves caught up in the net of bloodthirsty politics. Their greatest need was for a patron powerful enough to offset the local authority of the Duke of Norfolk. They found one in the Earl of Oxford. This put the Paston brothers in a good position, but it took them into war. When the battle lines were drawn the Earl called on the Paston brothers John II and III to fight under his standard and they could hardly refuse, even though it meant their taking a stand against the King when Oxford joined Warwick's rebellion. Thus the Pastons both fought in the Battle of Barnet in 1471. Unfortunately they ended up on the losing side when King Edward emerged victorious, Warwick was killed, the Earl of Oxford fled abroad and John III was wounded by an arrow in the elbow.

John III recovered, but the two Paston brothers had risked all. They were declared traitor by King Edward, with the likelihood of their possessions being confiscated, as was their uncle William Paston whose own royal connections were complicated by his Beaufort wife, daughter of Edmund Beaufort, Duke of Somerset, the Beauforts being distinctly out of favour at this time. Their defeat at Barnet might mean that all the Paston efforts to solidify their estates had gone for nothing. An anxious wait developed to see what would happen even though John II was 'betrothed' to Mistress Anne Haute, cousin of the Queen. They were fortunate that a royal pardon was offered, Edward IV needing all the friends he could get. Their estates were restored, but the ever lingering problem of Caister Castle was not solved.

It has to be said however that the Pastons were not without a wily plan, on or off the battle field. How to get Caister back without a battle and with a patron who was in exile? The death of the Duke of Norfolk presented an un-looked for opportunity.

The widowed Duchess of Norfolk was brought to bed of her second child at Framlingham Castle. John III who had held a position in the Norfolk household in his youth, attempted to persuade his mother Margaret to visit the Duchess and offer her services during the birth, Margaret having survived seven births. It was John III's plan that his mother persuade the ailing Duchess to give Caister back.

Whether Margaret actually attended this event is unclear. She may have done so. If so, did the two women discuss such business dealings while the Duchess was in labour? I doubt it. The Duchess gave birth to a son who died almost immediately, leaving a young daughter as the heir

to the Norfolk acres. Whether these two intrepid women had any effect on the fate of Caister, in May of that year the Royal Council at last pronounced in favour of the Pastons and the Duchess renounced it. Caister Castle belonged to Sir John II Paston and its ownership was never again questioned. It is encouraging to think that the work of women might have had an effect rather than warfare.

The Pastons were not always reluctant to pick up arms if it might play to their advantage. In early 1475 all five of the Paston brothers, sons of John I Paston, enlisted to fight under King Edward in the manoeuvring between England, France and Burgundy. England and Burgundy were in alliance against France and it seemed that war would ensue. In fact war was averted and the Paston brothers returned home without shedding any blood, either French or their own. At least they had proclaimed their loyalty to the King.

During the final years of English unrest, the Pastons found it politic to keep their heads down. There was no direct Paston involvement in the Buckingham rebellion or the events that led to the death of Richard III and the crowning of King Henry VII. John III kept a discreetly low profile, keeping clear of all conspiracies. John was presented with three dangerous possibilities: to fight for his old patron the Earl of Oxford on one side; to fight for the Duke of Norfolk on the other side; or to sit tight and do neither. John wisely chose to sit tight and await the outcome. Ultimately John III emerged from his political isolation to fight alongside the Earl of Oxford in the Battle of Stoke which put an end to the Lambert Simnel rising in 1487. As a reward for his conspicuous support John III was created Sir John Paston and Deputy Lord High Admiral. Their future was secure with the Tudors.

It is worth taking a final look at the fate of Elizabeth Paston, sister of John I Paston. She did not fare so well, her involvement in the Wars of the Roses being far more deadly. Her first husband Sir Robert Poynings survived involvement in Cade's rebellion, but then he fought in the Second Battle of St Albans for the House of York. He was killed on the battlefield, leaving his young son as heir and his estates in difficulty for Elizabeth, since they were claimed by his niece Eleanor through the complicated Kentish patterns of inheritance. Since this troublesome niece was wed

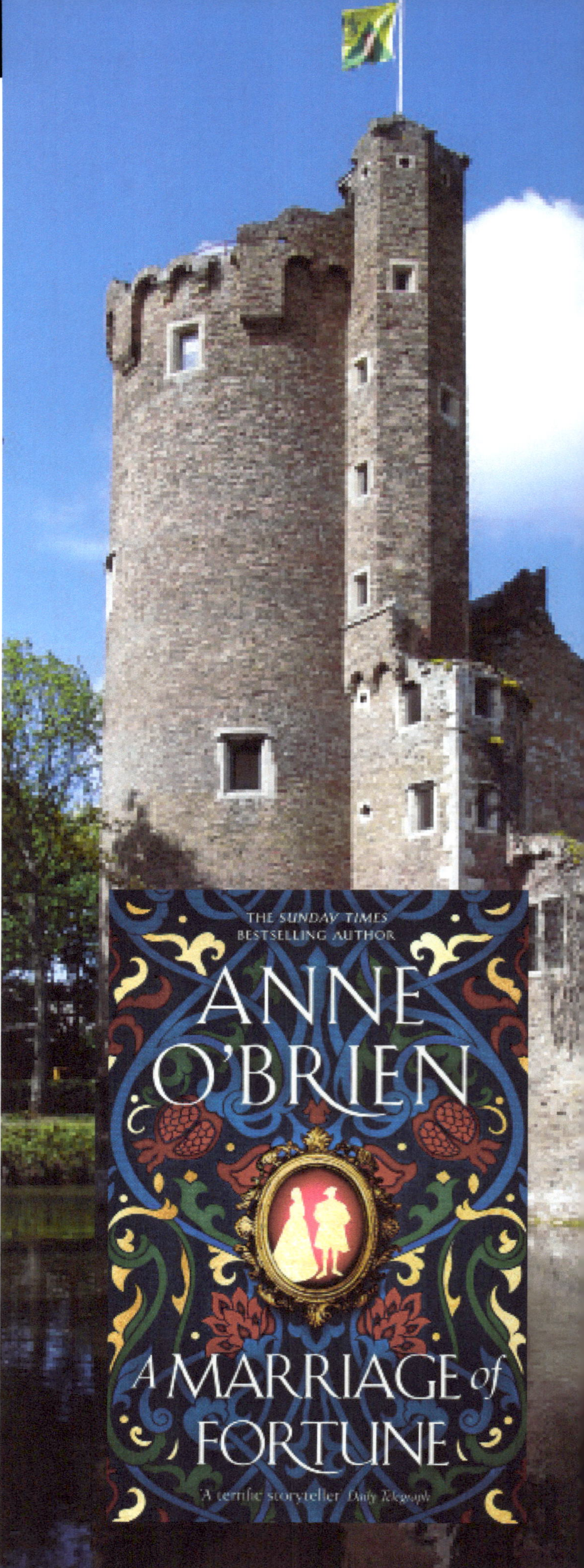

ANNE O'BRIEN

Anne was born in the West Riding of Yorkshire. After gaining a B.A. Honours degree in History at Manchester University, a PGCE at Leeds University and a Masters degree in education at Hull University, she lived in the East Riding as a teacher of history. Always a prolific reader, she enjoyed historical fiction and was encouraged to try her hand at writing. Success in short story competitions spurred her on.

Leaving teaching – but not her love of history – she wrote her first historical romance, a Regency, which was published in 2005. This was followed by nine historical romances and a novella, ranging from medieval, through the Civil War and Restoration and back to Regency, all of which have been published internationally.

Since then Anne has sidestepped historical romances to write about the silent women of medieval history. As Virginia Wolfe once said: 'For most of History, Anonymous was a Woman.' For this reason, she decided to shake the cobwebs from some of these medieval women of interest and allow them to take the stage, three-dimensional and with much to say.

Her new novel for September 2021 concerns the remarkable women of the Paston family who allowed us to see so much of their lives and their menfolk through their letters.

to the Percy Earl of Northumberland, she had far more influence than Elizabeth Paston. Elizabeth had to fight to keep the Poynings estates for their son Edward, a struggle for possession that dogged her for the rest of her life.

Nor did her second husband bring any light relief for her. This was Sir George Browne who survived the battle of Tewkesbury on the side of the Yorkists but then became involved with the Kentish rebels in the Buckingham Rising against Richard III in the first year of his reign. Browne was captured when the rebellion failed, tried for treason as one of the leaders of the rebellion in Kent, and was executed on Tower Hill, leaving the Browne estates also in jeopardy. Elizabeth's Poynings son Edward also joined the rebels and was forced to flee, joining the exiled Henry Tudor in his bid for the throne. Some women had much to suffer in wartime, but to Elizabeth's ultimate satisfaction, Edward returned to England to become a notable member of the Court of King Henry VII. Her son with Sir George Browne was also restored to his estates with the coming of the Tudors.

The Pastons were not one of the major 'mover and shaker' families in the Wars of the Roses, drawn as they were into the fighting against their wishes. They were men of law rather than men of the sword, but they emerged in good order. Their value to historians is of course their comment in their letters. We are give a splendid bird's eye view of how these middling families survived and managed to turn events to their own interests.

Anne now lives with her husband in an eighteenth century timber-framed cottage in the depths of the Welsh Marches in Herefordshire, a wild, beautiful place on the borders between England and Wales, renowned for its black and white timbered houses, ruined castles and priories and magnificent churches. Steeped in history, famous people and bloody deeds as well as ghosts and folk lore, it has given her inspiration for her writing. Since living there she has become hooked on medieval history.

Sometimes she escapes from writing. She enjoys her garden, a large, rambling area where she grows vegetables and soft fruit as well as keeping control over herbaceous flower borders, a wild garden, a small orchard and a formal pond. With an interest in herbs and their uses, Anne has a herb patch constructed on the pattern of a Tudor knot garden and enjoys cooking with the proceeds. Gardening is a perfect time for her to mull over what she's been writing, as she wages war on the weeds.

LEARN MORE at www.anneobrienbooks.com or at HarperCollins Publishers

MONARCHY, ARISTOCRACY, & DEMOCRACY

ELIZABETH ST. JOHN

"The land was then at peace (it being towards the latter end of the reign of King James), if that quietness may be called a peace, which was rather like the calm and smooth surface of the sea, whose dark womb is already impregnated with a horrid tempest."

So wrote Lucy Hutchinson in 1674, as one of the first English women diarists of the early modern age. In her retrospective Memoirs of the Life of Colonel Hutchinson, she described the halcyon setting of her beloved country in 1620, the year she was born…

"Britain hath been as a garden enclosed, wherein all things that man can wish, to make a pleasant life, are planted and grow in her own soil, and whatsoever foreign countries yield, to increase admiration and delight, are brought in by her fleets."

…commending the system of government in those idyllic days…

"Better laws and a happier constitution of government no nation ever enjoyed, it being a mixture of monarchy, aristocracy, and democracy, with sufficient fences against the pest of every one of those forms—tyranny, faction, and confusion;"

…until we catch the first glimpse of her rebellious spirit.

"Yet is it not possible for man to devise such just and excellent bounds, as will keep in wild ambition, when princes' flatterers encourage that beast to break his fence, which it hath often done, with miserable consequences both to the prince and people; but could never in any age so tread down popular liberty, but that it arose again with renewed vigour, till at length it trod on those that trampled it before."

Lucy Hutchinson was a dutiful wife, a highly educated and devout woman with a contempt for the practices of privilege and perquisites, royal prerogative, and a monarch's divine right to rule. She was that most dangerous of creatures: a revolutionary, who fought with words not swords, to leave us a firsthand account of England's most turbulent times, the seventeenth century. Along with her husband Colonel John Hutchinson, Lucy stirred the dangerous currents of resistance, creating a brewing tempest in the calm, smooth surface of Jacobean England.

While Lucy was sharing her brother's tutors and living in the Tower of London, where her Calvinist father was the keeper and her herbalist mother cared for the prisoners, her Aunt Barbara St. John was giving her own offspring a very different upbringing. Marrying into the ambitious Villiers family, she was quickly embroiled in a power-hungry syndicate that conspired to seduce the susceptible James I with a new favourite courtier. Barbara's brother-in-law, George Villiers, was a devastatingly attractive young man, with a face "as beautiful as St. Stephen" and a great pair of legs. To King James, he was an irresistible adornment to his inner court, and George quickly became the king's favourite, and remained so until James's death. As a result, Barbara and her husband Edward Villiers were showered with patronages and advantageous

positions, including the monopoly for gold and silver thread and an appointment as Master of the Mint. Even beyond Edward's early death, Barbara maintained her widow's privileged interests in these lucrative businesses for the rest of her life and never remarried.

There was a marked contrast between Lucy and Barbara's lives; for while Lucy's father purchased his position as Lieutenant of the Tower because of the Villiers' relationship, the similarities ended there. Although no doubt a shrewd businesswoman, there is no evidence of Barbara's academic achievements, nor were her children mentioned as being highly educated, except for the right of passage to attend Oxford University. On the other hand, Lucy's upbringing was highly intellectual:

"By the time I was four years old I read English perfectly, and having a great memory, I was carried to sermons; and while I was very young could remember and repeat them exactly…when I was about seven years of age, I remember I had at one time eight tutors in several qualities, languages, music, dancing, writing, and needlework; but my genius was quite averse from all but my book…and every moment I could steal from my play I would employ in any book I could find, when my own were locked up from me. My father would have me learn Latin, and I was so apt that I outstripped my brothers who were at school, although my father's chaplain, that was my tutor, was a pitiful dull fellow."

While Lucy was poring over her books and cultivating her revolutionary ideas of Calvinism and parliamentary government, her Aunt Barbara lived a privileged life at court. Edward Villiers and his brother, by now the Duke of Buckingham, enjoyed all the trappings of the highest level of aristocracy (as well as the more profitable benefits afforded them by their monopolies and mint activities). From James I's love of masques and hunting to his son Charles I's adoration of art and music, the Villiers' family made the most of the unlimited resources at their courtly fingertips. Such was the splendour in which they lived, they had no desire to pay attention to the inhabitants of England's "enclosed garden". So ensconced were they within the Stuarts, that when James I died and the crown passed to his heir, Charles I, the Duke of Buckingham smoothly transferred his devotion from father to son, and his privileged life continued uninterrupted. Courtiers such as the Villiers lived within a privileged bubble and ignored the unpleasant rumblings from increasingly verbose members of parliament that heralded storms on the horizon.

Away from London's opulent palaces, other women in Lucy and Barbara's family were considering broader prospects. Perhaps the boundless East Anglian fenlands and wide arching skies encouraged open thinking and infinite possibilities; the location was the centre of puritanical thinking and parliamentarian support. Elizabeth St.John was born into the senior branch of the aristocratic family living at Bletsoe Castle, Bedfordshire, on the edge of the fens. The daughter of a respected Elizabethan knight, she was the younger sister of Sir Oliver St.John, England's future Lord Chief Justice, parliamentarian leader against the king, and mastermind behind England's civil war.

Elizabeth grew up in an environment where women were educated and encouraged to think and speak for themselves, and by the time she was twenty-five she had married a charismatic preacher from King's Lynn, Norfolk, named Samuel Whiting. After generating a passionate and loyal congregation, they boarded a ship for New England in 1636, spearheading the wave of puritan emigrants seeking new horizons. Forging the folkways of East Anglia in their religion, customs, social mores, place names, and ideas of representational justice, they also carried the seeds of rebellion that were sprouting in their homeland. In their newly formed colony of Massachusetts, and their eponymously named town of Lynn, these radical ideas took root and thrived. Elizabeth and Samuel established their lives in New England and a hundred and forty years later, their social construct was harvested into fodder for America's own revolution. Elizabeth's generational quest for religious choice, along with freedom from tyranny and taxation by a dictatorial one-person government, had founded a new country.

Barbara Villiers
Dutchess of Cleveland
& Daughter to William
Villiers Viscount
Grandison

By the middle of the 1600s, England had squarely divided itself into several factions—those supporting the monarch and his "divine right to rule", those who favoured a parliamentary system with representation of the people, and a third, smaller group, of "independents" who thought there might be a hybrid solution.

Enter, now, a fourth St.John cousin—Anne Wilmot, wife of Henry Wilmot, a charismatic and highly beloved Royalist cavalier. As Charles I declared civil war in 1642, the Wilmots and the Villiers took up arms with the king, while Lucy Hutchinson along with Oliver St.John and his daughters favoured Parliament. Lucy Hutchinson's fear of a "horrid tempest" had arrived. As a result, the family divided along their passionately held beliefs, and in the ensuing seven years of civil war, they joined the bitterly fought battle between king and parliament, until, in Lucy's own words…"liberty arose again with renewed vigour, till at length it trod on those that trampled it before." The Royalist cause was lost, and Lucy Hutchinson's husband, John Hutchinson, was one of the regicides that authorised the execution of King Charles, thus ending the reigning monarchy in Britain.

During the Commonwealth years (1649-1660), Anne Wilmot maintained a Royalist household in the heart of Parliamentarian England and spent much of time her "befuddling" Cromwell's men from sequestering her home, as well as sending supplies and money to the exiled court in France. Simultaneously, Sir Oliver St.John, now Lord Chief Justice of England, was seeking a diplomatic solution to repair the divided nation, and although he effectively led Cromwell's government, he considered himself an independent. In the early 1650s, he married two of his daughters to their cousins, Anne's younger brothers. By uniting in marriage, the opposing branches of the St.John family demonstrated that families who were once foes could live harmoniously under Cromwell's Protectorate.

And did Lucy Hutchinson's dream of a commonwealth last? Only for eleven years. By 1660, Oliver Cromwell had died, and despite the efforts of Sir Oliver St.John and other senior parliamentary leaders, the hybrid ideal of "king with parliament" was not embraced. In May 1660, Charles Stuart returned to the England he had fled as a teenage cavalier, to be welcomed back as king and duly crowned in Westminster. And who was at his side? Barbara Villiers, the granddaughter and namesake of Barbara St.John, firmly established as the

king's favourite mistress. Along with her cousin John Wilmot, Earl of Rochester, long-suffering Anne's renegade son, these charismatic and dissolute family members set the tone for the roistering, decadent and pleasure-seeking two decades that were to mark the restoration of England's monarchy.

With Charles's return, the regicides who had executed his father were rounded up and executed, except for a handful who escaped to America, and Colonel John Hutchinson, Lucy's husband. By the intervention of two of Lucy's Royalist cousins—Anne Wilmot and Barbara Villiers, who pled leniency to the king and his council, stating that John had actually been helping the Royalist cause—John was pardoned.

"These are to certify that about seven years ago, and from time to time ever since, Colonel Hutchinson hath declared his desire of the king's majesty's return to his kingdoms, and his own resolutions to assist in bringing his majesty back: and in order thereunto hath kept a correspondency with some of us, when designs have been on foot for that purpose; and hath upon all occasions been ready to assist and protect the king's friends in any of their troubles, and to employ all his interests to serve them. He gave the Earl of Rochester notice and opportunity to escape when Cromwell's ministers had discovered him the last time he was employed in his Majesty's service here in England. He received into his house, and secured there, arms prepared for the king's service, well knowing to what intent they were provided, and resolving to join with us when there had been occasion to use them."

Anne Wilmot, Countess of Rochester

His health broken by imprisonment, Colonel John Hutchinson died in 1664, leaving Lucy a grieving widow determined to honour the memory of her beloved husband. She had kept diaries throughout the Civil War years and used those to write the Memoirs—— the extraordinary eyewitness account of an educated woman living through the tumultuous England revolution. Though the precious notebooks were too incen-

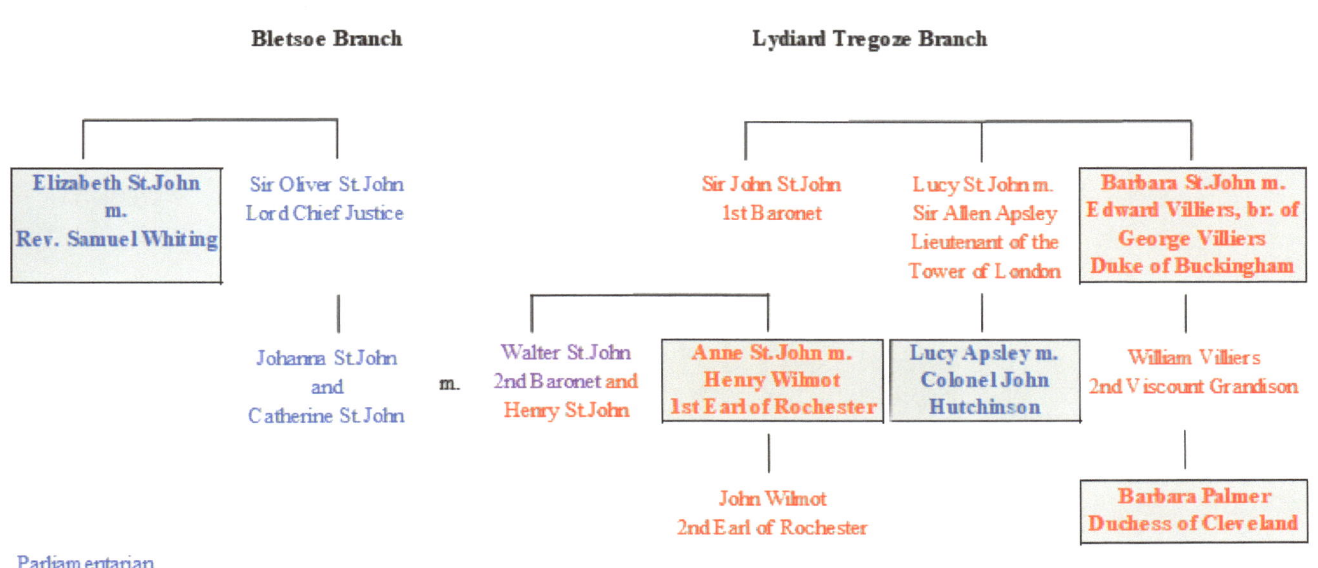

diary to publish in her lifetime, parliamentarian Lucy Hutchinson entrusted the precious diaries to Anne Wilmot for safekeeping. A descendent subsequently published the work in the following century.

Perhaps it's fitting to finish where we started—with the Barbaras who saw so much change and extraordinary social upheaval in their lifetimes. From the magnificent European art collections and spectacular architectural styles emerging under the patronage of Charles I and the Duke of Buckingham, to Charles II's extravagant French influences and profligate pleasure-seeking, England witnessed a flourishing in the arts, sciences, music, theatre, architecture, exploration, and commerce. Wars were fought and lost, commercial expansion created trade routes around the globe, and a reimagined government and monarchial working relationship was in place. Women such as Margaret Cavendish, Aphra Behn and Lucy Hutchinson were published, irrevocably opening the doors for women's voices to be heard and read, and not forgotten or dismissed.

Most significantly, the turmoil of Lucy Hutchinson's revolution created a society where people did imagine—and create—a new interpretation of world order, whether on distant shores or in their own "garden enclosed". By the end of the seventeenth century in Britain, a monarchy and aristocracy lived under the scrutiny of a representative parliament. In the New World, democracy was strengthening, and by 1775 a new "horrid tempest" erupted; another civil war that germinated the American Revolution.

Learn more about
Elizabeth St. John
and her books at
www.elizabethstjohn.com or at
www.thefriendsoflydiardpark.
org.uk

Victorian Britain demonised Emma Hamilton as an evil temptress who'd led their great hero, Lord Nelson, astray. However, her true tale is extraordinary. Born in proverbial rags, her genuineness and creativity changed the world forever, though society destroyed her reputation as soon as it could. Her story begins in a provincial English coal mining village, passes through childhood sexual exploitation, sees her instigating a worldwide fashion revolution and forging bosom-buddy friendships with international royalty, and then plummets into debt, depression and death.

Emma, baptised Amy, was born on 26th April 1765 in a village called Ness, near Liverpool in north-west England. Her father, a mine's blacksmith named Henry Lyon, died when she was two months old. She grew up with her mother's family eight miles away in Hawarden, north-east Wales. Their thatched cottage was next door to a public house called the Fox and Grapes. Her widowed grandmother scraped a living as a carter carrying coal. 18th century Britain was rigidly segregated by gender and class so young Amy had limited options ahead of her.

Her mother left Hawarden to work in London when Amy was twelve or thirteen. The young teen remained with her grandmother and gained employment of her own as a nurserymaid for the family of Dr Thomas. Her earliest known portrait was sketched by Dr Thomas's daughter and shows Amy in striking profile with an aquiline nose and large, dreamy eyes. Amy was taught basic literacy and numeracy by Mrs Thomas, but she had her heart set on the glamour of becoming an actress in London. She secured brief employment as a costume hand in London's Drury Lane and then, after a succession of short-lived jobs, like countless other country girls, made ends meet by selling her charms. An aristocrat employed her as his live-in mistress but threw her out when she became pregnant.

Amy begged help from Charles Greville, a friend of the aristocrat who'd abandoned her. Greville agreed to take her in if she gave up both her child and her wanton ways. He renamed her Emma Hart, and she excelled so well under his tutelage in deportment that the Audrey Hepburn musical, *My Fair Lady*, is based on their story. When sixteen-year-old Emma gave birth in the spring of 1782, her baby was sent to the care of her grandmother in Hawarden. Greville chivvied Emma to sit for his artist friend, George Romney who produced fifty paintings of her. In these days before social media, mass-printed copies of her portraits made her a celebrity.

Despite the public's craving for prints of Emma, Greville had become tired of her and sent her to his elderly uncle, Sir William Hamilton as a "clean comfortable woman" to enjoy in his British Ambassadorial bed in Naples. When she arrived on her twenty-first birthday, Sir William lavished her with luxuries, but it took her several months to realise she was expected to be his lover. She was furious and heartbroken that Greville had cast her off, but made the best of things and extended her education to drawing, music, singing and languages, which she accomplished to such high degrees that her Italian became fluent and she was offered £6,000 to be prima donna for the Italian opera in Madrid. Emma invented an entirely new art form, her "Attitudes", that comprised quick-fire poses depicting classical scenes. Her Attitudes became a must-see attraction for wealthy people during their Grand Tour of Europe. Her loose-fitting, Ancient Grecian-inspired getup drew artists to her like a magnet, making her one of the most painted women of her time. Fashion-minded ladies cast off their tall, powdered wigs in favour of dressing "à la Emma" (think "Jane Austen" fashion).

Emma's natural grace, warmth and charity endeared her to the people of Naples. A nun in a convent she regularly visited said she was like an angel, but snobbish Brits were less impressed. Lady Holland wrote scathingly of Emma's uncultured north-western English accent and Lady Elgin — whose husband is remembered for helping himself to marble sculptures from Athens's Parthenon — described Emma as "very vulgar". British society was scandalised when Sir William married her on 6th September 1791, not because he was sixty and she was twenty-six, but because aristocrats weren't supposed to wed commoners.

Although rooted in genuine affection, Emma and Sir William's marriage was mutually beneficial: she secured social status and he, as British Ambassador to Naples, gained a crucial diplomatic advantage. Na-

ples was a strategically important ally in Britain's war against revolutionary France. Being a man, Sir William was only permitted to approach the king, who had no interest in politics. It was the queen, Maria Carolina, who ran the state and Emma, now married, could be introduced to her. Emma and the queen became so intimate that rumours spread that they were lesbians. When Queen Maria Carolina learnt that her brother-in-law, Charles IV of Spain, was urging her husband to align with France she was horrified because the French had executed her sister, Marie Antoinette. Emma, who'd visited Marie Antoinette in prison in Paris, was equally horror-stricken. They collaborated to smuggle copies of Charles of Spain's letters to the British as important war intelligence.

In the summer of 1798, the commander of Naples-ruled Sicily refused Captain Horatio Nelson the supplies his ships needed to chase Napoleon's fleet to Egypt. Nelson wrote to Sir William begging help and Emma persuaded the queen to go behind the king's back to command the supplies to be released. Duly reaching The Nile, Nelson used strategic lateral thinking to obliterate the French. Anti-Napoleonic Europe was ecstatic when they heard of his victory; not least Emma who greeted his arrival in Naples from Egypt dressed head to toe "à la Nelson… with gold anchors all over", and exclaimed, "Oh God is it possible? and fell into his arms more dead than alive." In England, fashion-conscious women quickly copied her by wearing "gold anchors that celebrated their hero". Nelson was now an international superstar like Emma.

Nelson luxuriated with the Hamiltons, recuperating from battle wounds whilst the war raged on. Emma was deeply moved to hear that the people of Malta, caught between Britain and France, were starving. She "sent off three ships, laden with corn, and got £7,000 from the Queen, and gave 500 ounces of [her] own to relieve them." Tsar Paul of Russia, Grand Master of the Maltese Knights Hospitaller, responded by awarding Emma the Maltese Cross, making her the first British Dame of Malta.

When the revolutionary tide crashed into Naples in 1799, Emma helped the royal family sneak onto Nelson's flagship Vanguard for evacuation to Sicily. Nelson had become so intimate with the Hamiltons that they named themselves Tria Juncta In Uno (three joined as one). Nelson and Emma's famous romance seems to have begun in February 1800. Orders were issued for Nelson and Sir William to return to England, but Nelson delayed their departure by hijacking a British ship of the line to take the Hamiltons on a pleasure cruise around Malta. Nelson's superior, Lord Keith raged at his unsanctioned use of a valuable British warship and refused to permit another for their homeward journey so they traveled to England overland with cheering crowds following them in their thousands.

Nelson was cheered just as enthusiastically by the people of England when he and the Hamiltons landed at Great Yarmouth in England in November 1800. Emma, however, was mocked for being fat and the British queen refused to receive her. Nelson's wife, Fanny was overjoyed by his return, but he publicly slighted her in favour of Emma and moved in with the Hamiltons.

Emma gave birth to Nelson's daughter, Horatia in January 1801. Prudish society would have shunned both Emma and their illegitimate baby, so they pretended they'd adopted Horatia from one of Nelson's crewmen. It's probable that Sir William was discreetly aware of Horatia's parentage. The bonds between the Trio Juncta In Uno were deep. When Sir William died in 1803, he was in Emma's arms with Nelson holding his hand.

Nelson's family flocked to Merton Place where Emma lavished them with hospitality. Naval duty kept Nelson away until the summer of 1805. Nelson, Emma and four-year-old Horatia spent an idyllic August together there, only for the Admiralty to call Nelson away again in early September.

Church bells rang joyously across England on 6th November 1805 after news arrived of Nelson's obliteration of the combined French and Spanish fleets at Trafalgar. But Emma's heart was broken because Nelson had been killed in action. The government barred her from Nelson's funeral, which is thought to have been the biggest public event London had ever seen. Generous grants were awarded to Nelson's siblings and estranged wife and making his brother, Reverend William Nelson an earl, though Nelson's only dying wish had been for the British government to financially support Horatia – whose paternity he acknowledged – and Emma, in recognition of her war services, but they refused to pay them a penny.

Nelson had left what little he had to Emma and Horatia, including Merton Place, but their stipends were administered by William Nelson who'd shunned Emma as soon as the tide of public feeling turned and consistently delayed paying the stipends Nelson had bequeathed.

Although society demonised Emma as a man-using harlot, she had no heart to take any man after Nelson. Instead, she spent a fortune she didn't have hosting rich allies, including the future George IV, in the hope that they'd support her claim for a state pension. But she no longer had it in her to sparkle as a hostess, and all she accrued were debts and a drinking habit. She was forced to sell Merton Place in 1809.

Emma was confined to debtor's prison in 1812, then again in 1813. Friends bailed her out, but William Nelson had now entirely stopped paying her stipends from Nelson's will and debtors were once more closing in. She sneaked onto a boat to Calais with Horatia in July 1814 but new debts mounted in France. Emma died on 15th January 1815 with only teenage Horatia at her side.

Despite being poor-born and dying spurned and penniless, Emma changed the world. Her mastery of upper-class deportment inspired the musical *My Fair Lady*. She invented an entirely new art form, her Attitudes, which people flocked to see. She was responsible for the worldwide fashion revolution that's become associated with Jane Austen. She was the first British Dame of Malta, and Nelson always maintained that he'd not have achieved his pivotal Nile victory if Emma hadn't interceded with Queen Maria Carolina to supply his ships.

Lily Style is the direct descendant of famed lovers Admiral Lord Nelson and Emma Hamilton. A keen genealogist, her interest is in piecing together the real human stories lying behind dry facts. She writes regularly for Nelson-related publications. *Horatia's Secret* is her first historical novel.

Lily is also the creator and webmaster of Emma Hamilton Society, whose purpose is to provide positive and deserved press to Dame Emma Hamilton (her correct title is Dame as she was awarded the Maltese Cross). Dame Emma Hamilton has been unfairly maligned because of prevailing sexism and snobbery: she had unwedded relationships (but not promiscuously) and spoke with a common accent.

Learn more about Lily Style and her books at
www.lilystyle.co.uk or
www.emmahamiltonsociety.co.uk

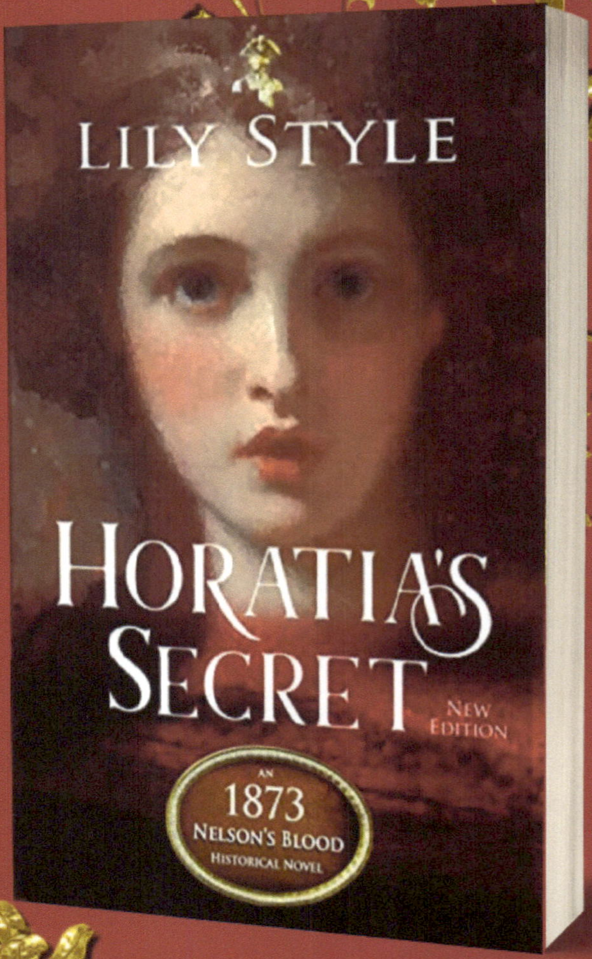

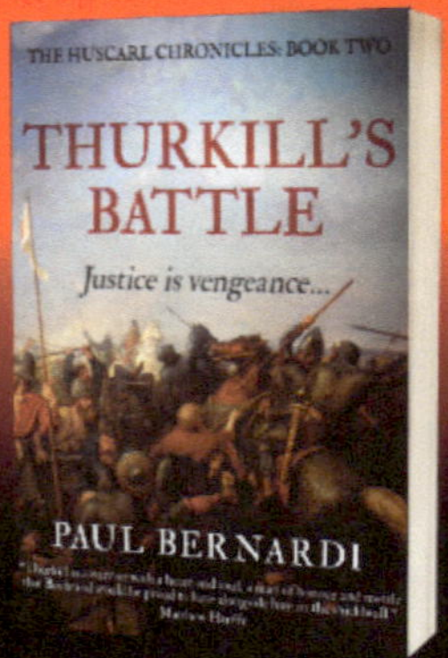

Irish folklore is well known around the globe, with pots of gold hidden at the end of every rainbow, and shamrocks and leprechauns abounding on St. Patrick's Day parades as famous landmarks worldwide are tinted green. The United States is no exception, with many Irish traditions long since an integral part of American culture—not least of all having a pint at an Irish pub!

Irish history is steeped in legend, fascinating young and old alike with stories of fairies and other mythical creatures, mysterious druids, and long-gone civilizations. But it's not just these magical aspects of Ireland's past that have caused its folklore to become so widely known, but rather the dispersal from their native land of hundreds of thousands of Irish people who brought their traditions with them to their new homes around the world.
The greatest of such flights from Ireland occurred in the wake of an event so catastrophic that its effects are still visible today—the Great Famine of the 19th century that saw the nation starve as its staple food, the potato, was destroyed by blight.

A troubled land

Even long before the start of the Great Famine Ireland was a troubled land, a fact that was to have an enormous impact on the devastating effects of the Famine itself. For centuries Ireland was oppressed by the neighboring English, who forced many of the natives off their land. Despite numerous attempted rebellions, by the early 1800s the majority of the Irish population found themselves having to rent tiny plots of farmland for vast sums from their conquerors to survive. Most were so poor that they possessed little more than the clothes on their backs. The overwhelming poverty and the enormous contrast between the multitude of commoners and the wealthy few was so extreme that it shocked travelers to 19th century Ireland, even at a time when most of Europe's peasantry had very little. Making matters worse was that the largely Catholic populace of Ireland was at the mercy of a Protestant minority. Naturally, feelings of resentment simmered in the locals and unrest was common.

THE GREAT IRISH HUNGER

JULIANE WEBER

The humble potato

Potatoes were initially introduced to Ireland as a garden crop before becoming widespread as a rotational crop. The natives soon discovered that the nutritious potatoes were well suited to the island's damp climate, were easy to grow without the need for constant care and produced a sizeable bounty even on small pieces of farmland, with a yield of about six to eight tons per acre. These attributes meant that the root vegetable quickly became the staple food for the majority of Irish peasants, who only had access to small pieces of land to grow their families' sustenance.

And despite Ireland's deeply rooted problems, its population continued to grow, along with its dependence on the potato. It has been estimated that by 1845, about seven million tons of potatoes were consumed in Ireland each year, with adult males eating up to 6.3 kilos per day—an amount quite unimaginable by modern standards. Many Irish people ate little to nothing else, with over one and a half million individuals entirely dependent on potatoes for their survival before the arrival of the blight, and an additional three million largely dependent on the crop. It was this overwhelming dependence on a single food on the eve of the Famine that contributed to the horrendous loss of life that was to follow—although nobody could have predicted such an event.

Phytophthora infestans

Identified as the fungus Phytophthora infestans only years later, the blight arrived in Ireland in 1845, sweeping across the land and destroying potato plants at an alarming rate. Although seasonal variations in crop yield had always been part of life it soon became apparent that this devastation was anything but normal, with about one-third of Ireland's total potato harvest ruined that season.

Despite this, concerted local relief efforts meant that few lives were lost the first year of the Famine as the

peasants dealt with the poor harvest the way they'd always done. Unfortunately, the same was not possible the following year. By the autumn of 1846 Ireland's poor were already down to their last resources. When the fungus again wreaked havoc on the harvest, this time destroying more than three-quarters of the yield, the effect was devastating. With nothing to eat, hundreds of thousands of people across the Emerald Isle found themselves entirely
dependent on the goodwill of others.

The government's response

The response of the government to the Famine has been much debated, with some accusing the British of nothing short of genocide, believing they purposefully let the Irish people starve. Others are less harsh in their criticism, of the opinion that even the most heroic of actions would not have been sufficient to prevent the enormous loss of life that resulted from the potato blight. What is clear, though, is that the government's response was vastly inadequate either way.

Throughout the Famine many in power had a laissez-faire attitude, believing the Irish had brought this devastation upon themselves and therefore needed to deal with it themselves. Even during the worst years of the Famine, the British refused to stop food exports that supplied the British market. Enormous quantities of grains and other foodstuffs therefore continued to leave Irish shores, while the people who tended Ireland's fields were starving. Food transports soon had to be placed under heavy guard to prevent them from being overrun by the desperately hungry populace. What little food was available to buy was priced far beyond what Ireland's poor could hope to pay. And although the government attempted to make up for some of the lost potato harvest by importing grains from America, these arrived too late for countless Irish men, women, and children who were in dire need. During the Famine years, there were individuals and organizations in Ireland and elsewhere around the world who did try to help where they could, donating food and funds and spurring others to action, but none of these efforts were even nearly enough to make any substantial impact on the devastation. With little to no crops harvested from their own fields, no money to buy food elsewhere, and insufficient aid, thousands upon thousands of Irish people succumbed to hunger and disease, many ending up in mass graves as whole villages were wiped out. In desperation, thousands more risked the dangerous passage across the ocean to seek a better life for themselves and their families in unknown lands, ending up as far afield as North America and Australia.

An Ireland forever changed

Ireland's Great Hunger was to last for five long years, during which the potato harvest failed four out of five seasons. By the time the Famine was finally over, more

than a million people had died and over a million more had fled Irish shores, leaving the Emerald Isle utterly devastated. The population of Ireland was reduced by about one-fifth—a loss that hasn't been recovered to this day. An entire social class, the cottiers, had been destroyed, the Irish Gaelic language had been largely lost along with the dead and the emigrated, and the structure of Irish society had been permanently altered.

The mass exodus of Irish people from their native land continued during the decade following the Famine and even throughout the remainder of the 19th century. This exodus saw survivors settle in far-off lands around the globe, along with the Irish culture and folklore that is now widely known and loved. But when next celebrating St. Patrick's Day or enjoying a pint of Guinness wherever in the world we may find ourselves, we owe it to the victims of the terrible tragedy that was the Great Famine to remember Ireland's haunting past.

References:
Gray, Peter. The Irish Famine (New Horizons). Thames & Hudson Ltd, London, 1995.
Donnelly Jr, James S. The Great Irish Potato Famine. The History Press, Gloucestershire, 2010.
Bourke, Richard & McBride, Ian (editors). The Princeton History of Modern Ireland. Princeton University Press, New Jersey, 2016.
Connolly, SJ (editor). Oxford Companion to Irish History. Oxford University Press, Oxford, 2011.

DID YOU KNOW?

Many Americans have Irish roots, including a number of famous ones such as President Joe Biden, former president John F. Kennedy, musician Bruce Springsteen, and quarterback Tom Brady, to name a few. The ancestors of many Irish Americans would have left Ireland in the 19th century to escape the devastation of the Great Famine and arrived in the US with hardly any possessions to their name.

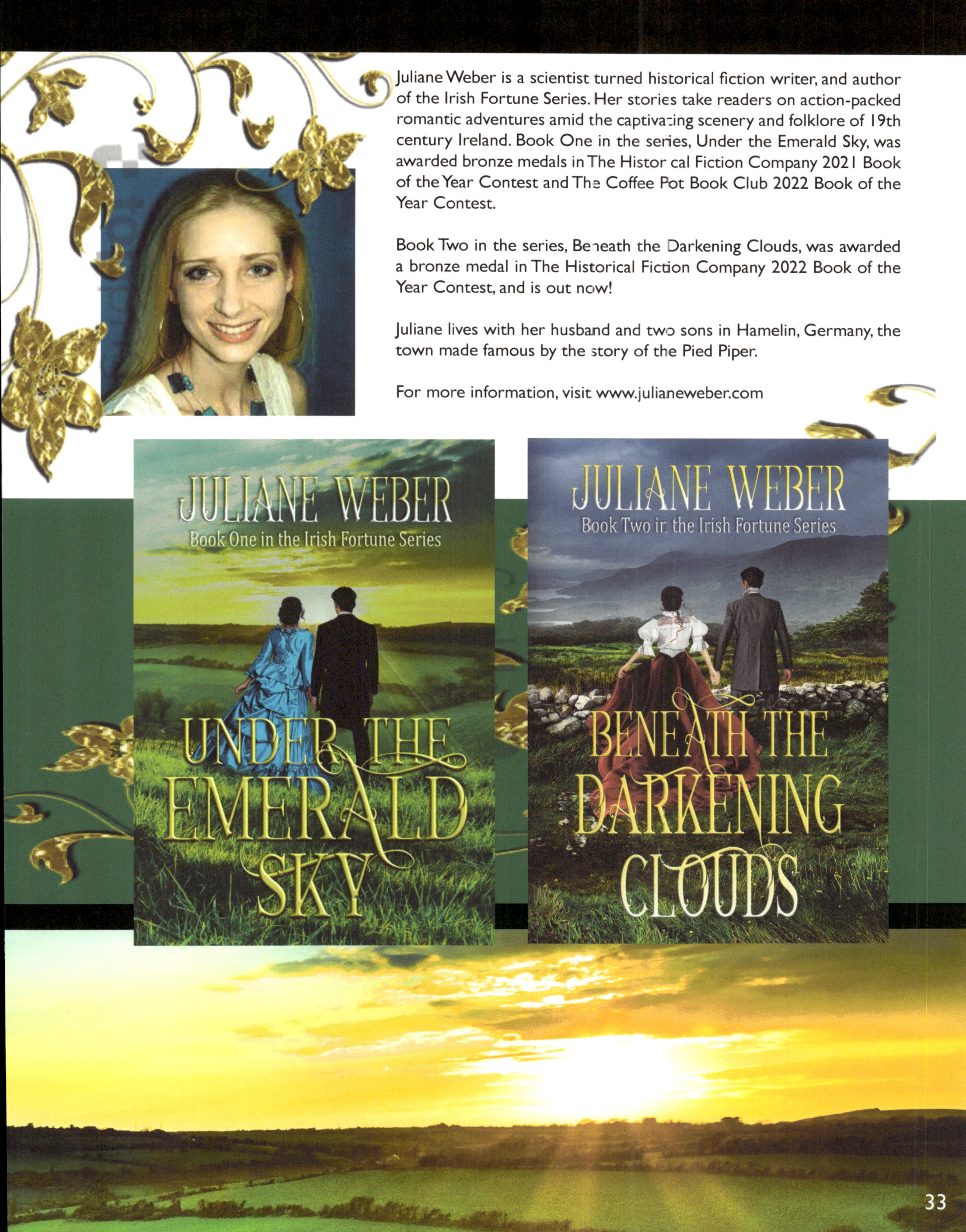

Juliane Weber is a scientist turned historical fiction writer, and author of the Irish Fortune Series. Her stories take readers on action-packed romantic adventures amid the captivating scenery and folklore of 19th century Ireland. Book One in the series, Under the Emerald Sky, was awarded bronze medals in The Historical Fiction Company 2021 Book of the Year Contest and The Coffee Pot Book Club 2022 Book of the Year Contest.

Book Two in the series, Beneath the Darkening Clouds, was awarded a bronze medal in The Historical Fiction Company 2022 Book of the Year Contest, and is out now!

Juliane lives with her husband and two sons in Hamelin, Germany, the town made famous by the story of the Pied Piper.

For more information, visit www.julianeweber.com

AN (IG)NOBLE SCOTTISH AFFAIR

D. G. MacDOUGALL

Rachel Erskine's peculiar story anticipates the modern-day whodunnit. A victim of scandal and conspiracy, she was violently kidnapped and held eighteen years in extremely harsh close-confinement. The ignoble perpetrators of this heinous crime came from the highest echelons of eighteenth-century Scottish society.

One of ten children of John and Margaret Chiesley of Dalry, outside Old Edinburgh, Rachel Chiesley was baptized February 4, 1679. Her childhood was singularly unhappy, overshadowed by an habitually abusive father. In 1689, the long-suffering mother filed a Letter of Separation and Aliment. Seventeenth-century Scottish divorce laws were relatively progressive; a woman could sue and aliment—or alimony—was permitted.

The judge, Sir George Lockhart of Carnwath, granted Margaret Chiesley a hefty aliment. John Chiesley was enraged—oddly, not with his estranged wife but, rather, with the judge. Chiesley vowed revenge and, on Easter Sunday, March 31, 1689, John shot Lockhart dead in an Edinburgh street. Within three days, Chiesley was convicted and hung at the Mercat Cross; the hand which fired the pistol was chopped-off, and the gun tied around his neck. Strangely, Chiesley's body was stolen that night; in 1825, a one-armed skeleton was found—a rusted pistol around its neck—under a countryside cottage hearthstone. "Johnnie One-Arm's" restless spirit is said to still haunt Dalry House.

In 1707, twenty-eight-year-old Rachel Chiesley encountered the Honorable James Erskine of Mar, a younger brother of John Erskine, Earl of Mar—the infamous "Bobbing John" of The 1715 Jacobite Rebellion. How Rachel and James became involved is puzzling. Given her relatively lower social status (and father's scurrilous past), Rachel was a dubious match for the up-and-coming lawyer and scion of an anciently noble house. Maybe simple physical attraction was all: Rachel Chiesley was reputed a "wild beauty" in her youth. Regardless, they married in August 1709 after Rachel became pregnant; over ten years they had eleven children.

James Erskine's law career progressed smoothly and rapidly in that time. Admitted Advocate in 1705, by 1707 he was a Lord of Justiciary—becoming Lord Grange—then promoted Lord Justice Clerk, in 1710, at just thirty years old.

Their wealth grew accordingly. The Erskine's owned a fine townhouse in Niddry's Wynd, just off Edinburgh's fashionable High Street, then acquired a country estate near Preston, Midlothian. Unusually, for a contemporary woman, James made Rachel the Factor of Preston, becoming solely responsible for the functioning of the property.

By 1718 cracks appeared in the Erskine's relationship. Rumors circulated that Rachel was demented, being "of a fierce revengeful temper, and a victim of intemperance," and also "jealous of all his [James Erskine's] irregularities" (Laing, 1874, p. 602). James Erskine, was a paradox: "a singular compound of good and bad qualities;--he was an acute and accomplished man as a lawyer, somewhat profligate in private life, yet with great pretensions to piety, restless and intriguing in political affairs…" (Laing, 1874, p. 602).

Lord Grange's private life was indeed profligate. Engaged in an affair with Fanny Lindsey, owner of a coffee shop in Edinburgh's Haymarket, Erskine simultaneously plotted against the Hanoverian regime in London. Rachel Erskine was greatly distressed by his extramarital and Jacobite dalliances.

Rachel was especially infuriated upon discovering James' mésalliance with the coffeehouse proprietor Fanny Lindsey—he retaliated by dismissing her as Factor of Preston. In April 1730, Lady Grange's private belligerence became public acrimony; in the street outside their townhouse, Rachel publicly proclaimed Lord Grange's adultery, also denouncing him—and his high-born co-conspirators—as treasonous Jacobites. She threatened to run naked and commit suicide in the street—and also slept with a razor under her pillow.

Unsurprisingly, Lord Grange, "took [such] an insuperable aversion to her that they agreed to live separately" (Spowart, 1877, p. 313). However, it was Rachel—not James—who acted. On July 27, 1730, she filed a Letter of Separation and Aliment, asking for "Household furniture and Linnings [linens] & Plate as you think fit for my service and use & I will instantly on your acceptance hereof retire from your House and fulfill what is above on your Honor." In return, she promised to "retire and live by my self" (Spowart, 1877, p. 313). However, Rachel would not leave James in peace. She was "a spy not only on her husband's course of life, but his political intrigues" (Spowart, 1877, p. 312).

The final straw was Rachel Erskine's interception of Lord Grange's treasonous correspondence. James resorted to his Jacobite cronies for help: Simon Fraser, eleventh Lord Lovat, Norman MacLeod, twenty-second of MacLeod, and Sir Alexander MacDonald, baronet of Sleat. Enlisting henchmen to do the dirty work, these canny men stayed at arms-length. When, in January 1732, Rachel announced she was taking James' damaging letters to London, the conspirators were forced to act.

The plot began January 22, 1732, the night before Rachel's London departure. Inexplicably, Lady Grange was staying with Lord Grange's next-door neighbor—but the quisling willingly invited the attackers inside. Rachel wrote, "there rush'd in to my room some servants of Lovats and his Couson [sic] Roderick Macleod he is writer to the Signet" (Laing, 1874, p. 602)—MacLeod was a lawyer and likely knew Lord Grange from court. Roderick gagged and threw Rachel to the bedroom floor; when she tore the gag out, "and told Rod: Macleod I knew him, rude hard hands abassd my face all below my eyes they dung [sic] out some of my teeth and…tore out some of my hair" (Laing, 1874, p. 602). Lady Grange was seriously injured, "all the linnius [linens] about me were cover'd in blood" (Laing, 1874, p. 603).

Rachel was fifty years old—elderly for her time— yet valiantly fought back. "I wrestled then defended myself" (Laing, 1874, p. 602), she wrote, "then Rod: ordered to tye down my hands" (Laing, 1874, p. 602). The kidnappers hustled the mangled lady into a waiting sedan chair; inside was Alexander Foster of Carsbonny who restrained Lady Grange as they escaped.

Simon Fraser, 11th Lord Lovat
Image from Wikipedia

Once outside the city, the feisty Rachel was tied over a horse saddle, "that I might not leope of [sic]." Roderick MacLeod, Peter Fraser—Lord Lovat's page—Alexander Foster, and one Andrew Leishman, took her west, arriving early morning at the house of "John MacLeod, advocate a little beyond Linlithgow" (Laing, 1874, p. 603). John MacLeod of Muiravonside, another lawyer, was Roderick's cousin—both were MacLeods of Berneray (Cameron, 1871, pp. 94-95). However, fearing outcry and pursuit from Edinburgh, they quickly departed Muiravonside House.

A cleit is a stone storage hut or bothy, uniquely found on the isles and stacs of St Kilda; whilst many are still to be found, they are slowly falling into disrepair. There are known to be 1,260 cleitean on Hirta and a further 170 on the other St Kilda-group islands. Image from Wikiwands.

The destination of the kidnapper's "cargo" (as MacDonald of Sleat called Rachel) (Laing, 1874, p. 602) was Wester Polmaise House, Stirlingshire; it was no coincidence that Alexander Foster was its Factor and Andrew Leishman the tenant. Upon arrival, Rachel wrote "they took me thro…a vault to a low room with all the windows nailed up and no light in the room he was soo [sic] cruel to leave me all aloan [sic] and two doors locked on me" (Laing, 1874, p. 603).

The kidnappers dropped the cargo and left. Foster, Leishman, and the estate gardener, George Rate, remained as jailers—Mrs. Leishman fed Rachel and washed her clothes. One day, Lady Grange, feigning sickness, was released from the dungeon. Encountering Rate, Rachel begged he send word to two church ministers, Hamilton and Erskine, whom she knew in nearby Stirling, that "I was Ld Grange Wife… and a prisoner in Pomeise [sic]…but it was all in vain" (Laing, 1874, p. 603). Rachel Erskine endured seven more months in Wester Polmaise's dank basement. Originally, she was to be committed to an insane asylum in Balquhidder, Perthshire, but it was deemed too public, so other plans were hatched.

On August 15, 1732, henchmen came to Wester Polmaise to take Rachel away, though she refused: "I had kept my bed all that day with grief and sorrow" (Laing, 1874, p. 603). The ruffians seized her, "and tho I was naked took me up by force and sett me up on a horse behind Mr Foster" (Laing, 1874, p. 603). They went westward to Loch Hourn where a ship waited; along the way inquisitive sight-seers viewed Lady Grange with curiosity—but none intervened. Roderick MacLeod, the chief kidnapper, reappeared at Loch Hourn and he sailed with Lady Grange, westerly to the Outer Hebrides.

On September 30, 1732, they reached the Heisker islands—the Monachs—five miles west of North Uist. Lord Grange's Jacobite associate, Sir Alexander MacDonald of Sleat, was the laird and his two tenants, Alexander MacDonald, and his wife—neither of whom spoke English—were the unwilling hosts. Rachel was now both physically and linguistically isolated.

Tacksman Alexander MacDonald pitied her: "after some time there he thought it was a sin to keep me he said he would let me go" (Laing, 1874, p. 603). A boat was hired but then the stranger "ran away with my money," stranding Lady Grange (Laing, 1874, p. 603). Rachel ungratefully berated the impoverished MacDonalds for their bad food, dirty clothing, and rundown shelter—though the Gaelic-speakers understood little. After two years, the fed-up MacDonalds begged that this demonic lady be taken away.

On June 14, 1734, a ship arrived in Heisker. John MacLeod, and his brother Norman MacLeod of Berneray, brothers of the ring-leader Roderick MacLeod, came to take Rachel even farther away. Crude as Heisker was, Rachel fought removal: "they were very rud [sic] and hurt me sore…my skin made black and blew" (Laing, 1874, p. 602).

Her new prison was MacLeod's island of Hirta, in the Saint Kilda archipelago, forty miles out into the Atlantic Ocean. Bleak and cliff-bound, it is sparsely populated—sheep outnumbering humans—with millions of screeching seabirds the only other company. Lady Grange lamented that "it is a viled neasty [sic] stinking poor Isle. I was in great misery in the Husker [Heisker] but I'm ten times worse and worse here [Hirta]" (Laing, 1874, p. 603). Solitary in a damp and dirty shack, she become overly-fond of Scotch whiskey. Despite all, Rachel remained determined to escape. Salvation came in the form of the Rev. Roderick MacLennan of Hirta who agreed to secretly forward a letter dated January 20, 1738.

In September 1740, Lady Grange's letter finally reached her Inverness lawyer Sir Thomas Hope of Rankeillor. Back in 1732, Hope was initially unconcerned: "After she was carried off, and being assured she was well entertained and cared for, I thought it was best not to move in that affair" (Laing, 1874, p. 605). Now, learning the shocking truth, Rankeillor organized a rescue mission.

On February 14, 1741, Hope, with twenty armed men, arrived at Hirta. But it was too late: Rachel had been spirited away the previous summer. She was taken ever deeper into MacLeod territory, yet Sir Thomas doggedly pursued his client until the trail went cold in 1742.

Lady Grange's final years were merciful, comfortably lodged with MacLeod's Skye tenants who buried her with dignity on May 12, 1745. Many years later, Dr Johnson sarcastically wrote of Lady Grange in Skye, "if M'Leod would let it be known that he had such a place for naughty ladies, he might make it a very profitable island!" (Boswell, 1785).

Lord Grange's career was unperturbed throughout. When Rachel first disappeared in 1732, James publicly claimed she died suddenly after a short illness; at her funeral a rock-filled coffin was interred. Fanny Lindsey, the mistress, then moved into Niddry's Wynd with James; they did not immediately marry, discretely waiting until December 1745—six months after Lady Grange's death. James Erskine, Member of Parliament, died in London on January 24, 1754.

Lady Grange's peculiar story reads like today's true-crime thrillers. Its wide-ranging conspiracy ensnared many at the highest levels of Scots society. Through their malign influence, rescuers were consistently stonewalled—or warned off—for eighteen incredible years. Equally scandalous is the lack of outcry upon Rachel's kidnapping—even her children were uninterested in their mother's fate. In the end, her story is also one of courage and resilience in the face of monstrous evils.

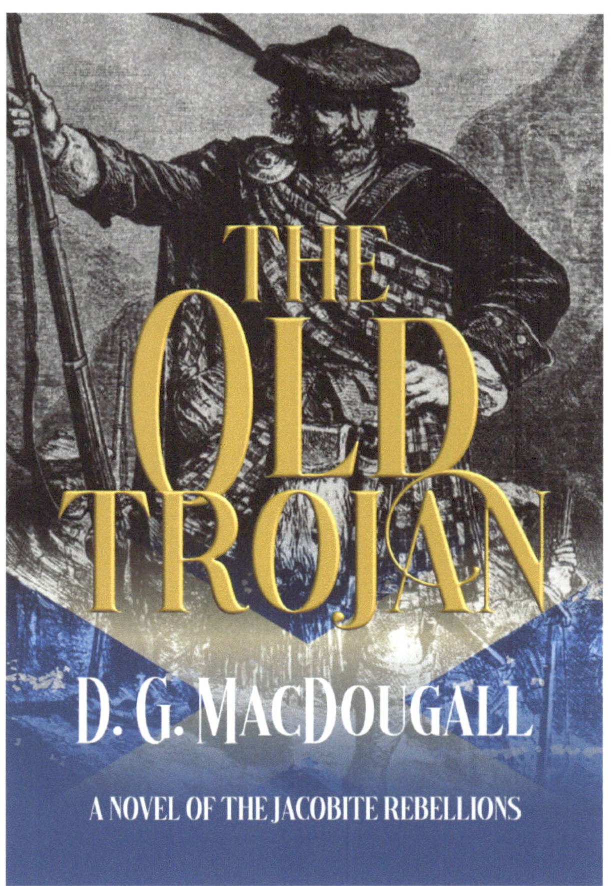

The Old Trojan, Donald MacLeod, the Laird of Unish and Bernera, was the last of his kind. A chieftain and commander of his clan during the Jacobite Rebellions, he defied his own chief and brought his MacLeods "out" for the Stuarts in 1715 and 1745. A noble descendant of the mighty Norse founders of the Clan MacLeod, Donnhuill mac Iain mac Tormod i'c Leoid—Donald, son of John, son of Norman MacLeod—was a Scottish warrior and leader without peer. Cast in the mold of the medieval Viking warlords who conquered the islands of Scotland's Western Hebrides, Donald MacLeod earned the epithet of The Old Trojan on the battlefields of Sheriff Muir, Falkirk, and Culloden. In his long life of eighty-plus years, The Old Trojan married three times, had twenty-six children, played a role in the mysterious disappearance of Lady Grange, was involved with the Ship of the People episode, and fought in the Seaweed Wars. Through it all, The Old Trojan witnessed and resisted the decline of the traditional Scottish clan system as the rebellions strained then broke the ancient and traditional bonds between clansmen and clan chiefs. Largely set in the chaotic period between the Glorious Revolution of 1688 and the Battle of Culloden in 1746, this is a lively account of one of the last of the Scottish warlords who would forever disappear with the coming of the Highland Clearances. Readers interested in the historic Scottish clans of the Hebrides, especially the MacLeods, will find in this novel a gripping tale, based on real people and events, of those chaotic times.

Visit Amazon.com to learn more about D. G. MacDougall's book.

THE MYTHS OF THE ISLE OF SKYE

GARETH WILLIAMS

The Isle of Skye is very popular these days. It is visited for its extraordinary scenery that ranges from collapsed ridges eroded into needles and old men and the remains of a massive caldera, a jagged curve of ridge that is all that remains of a giant volcanic explosion. The Cuillin hills demand respect. Sea lochs indent the coast so invasively that at one point, the width of the fifty-mile long island can be crossed in less than two hours of walking. Offshore are seals and whales, lobsters and scallops. There are fine places to eat, chic places to stay and plenty of serious weather to make everyone appreciate a bluebird day when the wind is in abeyance and the midges have yet to rise.

By one popular definition, a myth is a story passed down the generations explaining how or why something came to be; whereas a legend is designed to teach a lesson about a real person in history, although the facts may be dramatically altered. In this article I am going to examine an example of each that relates intimately to Skye. Firstly, I will relate the myth of the Fairy Flag. Secondly, I will recount the legend of Saucy Mary.

People have lived on the island since the Mesolithic era. There are standing stones, ancient monastic settlements and a castle that has been occupied by the same family for more than eight hundred years. Dunvegan Castle is, perhaps not surprisingly, the oldest continually occupied castle in Scotland. Home to the chief of the MacLeods, it sits defiantly on bedrock, its high, almost dour walls battered by Atlantic storms while its sheltered gardens blossom below.

But it is not just humans who have long called Skye home. Other folk have shared the Misty Isle with the MacLeods and MacDonalds since first tales were told huddled around firepits in caves or Black Houses. If you visit the castle, you can still see the fragile proof of an enduring understanding between fairies and humans. The Fairy Flag hangs on the wall of the castle between two ornate mirrors. Simply framed, it looks impossibly delicate, a torn and tattered remnant of an old alliance.

There are several tales about Am Bratach Sith that explain the flag's origin. They are all worthy of attention. Myth has it that the sacred banner is endowed with miraculous powers. Unfurled at the moment of greatest need, it would enable the clan to overcome impossible odds. The two traditional stories that credit fairies involve a tower and a bridge.

One night, there is a feast at the castle, braziers defying the dark. The clan chief's son is settled in his cradle by his nurse in a tower room. The nurse slips away to join the party in the keep. Meanwhile, the restless baby grizzles, kicking off his blanket and crying unheard. Unheeded that is until a fairy appears to comfort the child, wrapping him in a shawl of fine silk. When the nurse returns to her charge, he is gurgling contentedly, and when she carries him down in his fairy wrap, the room fills with unseen voices singing the Fairy Lullaby. Those swaddling clothes become the Fairy Flag.

Long before written records, a chief of the MacLeods married a fairy. They were together for a year and a day before the fairy had to return to fairyland. Their sorrowful parting took place at the Fairy Bridge near Dunvegan. As a memento, she gave the chief the banner and told him that whenever the clan was hardpressed in battle, flying it would deliver victory no matter how unlikely. With her final words she warned him that this magic could only be used three times.

In two major clan battles, the Fairy Flag was waved and saw the MacLeods triumphant. In 1939 it a major fire broke out but as the flag was being carried to safety, the wind died away and the flames abated. During the Second World War, pilots from the clan carried images of the flag to watch over them. Reputedly, Dame Flora MacLeod had the flag flown on the white cliffs of Dover to repel the inevitable German invasion.

The explanation that might persuade the sceptics who do not believe in the fairies of Skye, and who doubtless reject the claim that they shared the island with giants, dwarves, ghosts, kelpies, seers, Swan Folk and witches, suggests the flag came from the Holy Land. A MacLeod crusader struggles up to a mountain pass where he is given food and shelter by a hermit. The crusader listens as his host warns him of an evil spirit, the daughter of Thunder, that guards the pass. Unperturbed, the knight kills the spirit who, with her final breath foretells the future of the clan. She instructs him to take her girdle and have it made into a banner.

There is no point applying science to the first two legends. They require belief in a world far less certain than the one we think we occupy. However, the crusader version may be considered in light of the following information. Sir Reginald Macleod of MacLeod (27th Chief) had the Fairy flag conserved and placed in a sealed frame by the Victoria and Albert Museum. Their expert had a theory. The flag was likely woven from silk in the fourth century in either Syria or Rhodes. He drew a connection to the Norse king Harald Hardrada, a supposed ancestor of the MacLeod chiefs. The Norseman had led an expedition to plunder the pilgrim routes of the Middle East and brought back a renowned banner. If he flew this banner during his invasion of Britain, it was not yet imbued with magic, because he fell at the battle of Stamford Bridge.

I think the last word on the matter should go to Sir Reginald who told the expert, 'You may believe that, but I know that it was given to my ancestor by the faeries.'

At the end of the linear township of Kyleakin, once a busy place whenever the ferry from Kyle of Lochalsh called, but now much quieter since the narrows were spanned by the graceful Skye bridge, sits the increasingly ruined Castle Maol. In the twelfth century, this stronghold was home to a Norwegian princess, married to a MacKinnon. She was in the habit of extorting a toll from every passing ship, except those from her native land. It is alleged she had a chain run across the strait, some seven hundred metres at least! Why, then, you may ask was she dubbed Saucy Mary? One explanation has it that she would reward each dutifully paid toll with a flash of her bare chest as the ship sailed onwards!

Caisteal Maol ruins, Skye, Scotland - Wikipedia Commons

Further north, beyond Broadford but looming above it is Beinn na Caillich, literally, Hill of the Old Woman. Here too, the legend is of a Norse princess who, ever homesick, was buried beneath a great cairn atop the hill so that she might in death look towards the land she loved and feel the wind that once caressed Scandanavian shores. It is claimed that if she ever sees danger approaching, she will return to warn her descendants. I like to think these two princesses are one and the same.

Beinn na Caillich Summit - Wikipedia Commons

These two legends highlight a very real connection between Skye and Norway. Until the treaty of Perth in 1266 the island was regarded as under Norse control. The two clans who feature in the myths and legends above might reasonably be described as Norse-Gaels. Their allegiance to Norway was broken by the failure of King Haakon IV to decisively defeat the forces of Scottish King Alexander III at the Battle of Largs in 1263. The Norse fleet had anchored in the straits off Castle Maol on the eve of that battle. An indecisive encounter, it nevertheless marked the end of Norwegian overlordship as Haakon died before the end of the year.

Much of the highlands and islands remained a separate kingdom until 1493, ruled over by the Lord of the Isles. A title now held by the Duke of Rothesay, eldest son of the King of Scotland, and subsequently the King of Great Britain, at present Prince William. And thus we arrive at the present via myths, legends and a few incontrovertible historic facts. A present that sees Skye more popular than ever. Visitors treading in the footsteps of those most famous of tourists, James Boswell and Dr Johnson find, as they did, that 'the hospitality of this remote region is like that of the golden age'.

I was born in Essex in the UK and studied history at Queens' College, Cambridge which led to a career as a history teacher and school manager in Guernsey, Oxfordshire and Berkshire. Having retired, I moved to the magical Isle of Skye with my wife Helen and our seventh Pyrenean Mountain dog, a rescue called Sophie. I played rugby until I was forty-eight, and remain a passionate supporter of the Welsh national team. Despite breaking my back in a 400 foot fall down a mountain, I am working my way through all 282 Scottish mountains over 3,000 feet. I am also an ardent downhill skier and have recently taken up back-country and cross-country skiing. I am a keen member of the Skye Ravens mixed hockey team, usually playing in goal during matches.

THE VOYAGE OF SIR RICHARD EDGECOMBE INTO IRELAND IN 1488
POLITICAL COMMUNICATION AND RITUAL SYMBOLISM IN LATE MEDIEVAL ANGLO-IRISH RELATIONS

KATERINA DUNNE

'The Voyage of Sir Richard Edgecombe into Ireland' is a journal recording the mission of Sir Richard Edgecombe to Ireland in the summer of 1488. It was probably written by one of the men who accompanied Edgecombe while the latter negotiated the submission of the local Anglo-Irish lords in exchange for King Henry VII's pardon for those who participated in the Yorkist plot of 1487 to put impostor Lambert Simnel on the English throne. Although the source has been used by historians to establish a narrative of events, it has not been sufficiently explored for the specific information it provides on the various aspects of political communication.

This article will comment on 'The Voyage' as a valuable source on the way negotiations were conducted in late 15th century Anglo-Irish relations and on the significance of rituals and symbols in the public demonstration of political power and authority. A closer look at the text reveals that the behaviour of the main negotiating parties (Sir Richard Edgecombe and the Earl of Kildare) resembles a theatrical performance, where each action is carefully taken to make either party appear in a position of power.

Political Communication

Means of communication

Edgecombe communicated in person with those parties who were willing to submit promptly. However, in his negotiations with the Earl of Kildare (one of the most prominent supporters of the Yorkist plot) the communication between them was sometimes in person and sometimes through intermediaries. The daily entries in the journal reveal that after Edgecombe arrived in Dublin, envoys went back and forth between him and Kildare to deliver documents, ask for clarifications or to escort Edgecombe to meeting locations. Edgecombe attended in person only when deemed important for him to be present; for instance, when he delivered the King's message and demands, when he was invited to Kildare's residence as a guest, when he attended the lords' council to answer questions and offer clarifications, when he attended the oath-taking ceremony, and when he accepted the lords' certificates and handed the letters of pardon. In other non-essential situations, he sent documents and his views through intermediaries, and he was not present at the councils where the lords discussed their options and made their decisions.

The use of time as a negotiating device

From the start, the Earl of Kildare used delays and stalling. It took 27 days (4 – 30 July) for the two parties to reach an agreement. The repetition in the journal entries sounds tedious, but I believe this was done deliberately to demonstrate Edgecombe's frustration. Although the reasons for the delays (as provided in the text) are rather superficial, we can infer that Kildare was stalling in order to manipulate the outcome of the negotiations. He knew he had secured the King's grace, as Edgecombe had the pardon letters with

THE
VOYAGE
OF
Sir Richard Edgecomb,
Into IRELAND, in the Year 1488.
Collated with a M. S. of Dr. Swan, late Bishop
of Clogher, in the College Library.

Here Articulately setforth as well the Beginning
of the Voyage of Sir Richard Edgecomb, Kt.
send by the King's Grace into Ireland, and of
souche Communications, and Conclusions, as
the sayd Sir Richard hath made and takin
there, as also of his return agen into England.

THE 14th, 1488, Anno Septio Henry VII.
seyde Sir Richard took Shipping at Moun-
bay in Cornwall, in a Shipp called the Anne
Fenny allorsaid, and that were three other Ships
breaking upon him, with five Hundryth Men in charge
bey Strete, a Barque of Sir John Fyssh, Kt. and a Barque
of William Brewer, and that Daye he sailed to the Land's
End, and there rod at Anchor that Night, because the
Wind was contrary.

him, so he did not wish to be seen capitulating too soon. He was also aware that Edgecombe was eager to complete his mission quickly due to the expenses he was incurring and because he needed to return to the King as soon as possible. The timing of the death of the Scottish King put even more pressure on Edgecombe to secure the desired result. There is only one occasion when Edgecombe delayed the process. On July 20 he did not agree with rushing the oath-taking ceremony and deferred it until the next day. This shows that despite the time pressure, he was still cautious and did not wish to make hasty decisions.

Demands and concessions

The other technique the Earl of Kildare used to achieve better terms in the negotiation was the demands that he and the other Anglo-Irish lords made on Edgecombe for concessions. The most crucial one was that they would not accept the main sanction, which would be imposed on them if they violated their terms of submission. The text does not specify what this sanction, called 'bond of Misi', was. Some historians propose the bond concerned forfeiture of land while others suggest a financial penalty. The famous phrase that the lords would rather all become Irish than agree to the bond was probably not a serious threat, but this refusal made Edgecombe's position even harder. Despite his harsh words, Edgecombe showed enough flexibility to alter the terms in the end and accept an oath of allegiance sworn on the Sacrament. An additional demand to include Judge Plunkett and the Prior of Kilmainham in the King's pardon provoked a strong reaction from Edgecombe, but as this had come at the very last minute in the negotiation process, he was obliged to include Plunkett in the pardon in order to receive the lords' certificates and sureties as soon as possible. However, he showed firmness in his decision to exclude the Prior of Kilmainham. It seems they had finally found middle ground as Kildare did not make any further objections.

Communication with other parties

Separately from the main negotiation process, Edgecombe met numerous other parties (lords, bishops, mayors and prominent citizens) either for dinner or to take their oaths of loyalty. It is not certain whether these parties wished to distance themselves from the Earl of Kildare, but their eagerness to entertain Edgecombe and their willingness to submit promptly show that they were anxious to protect themselves by showing loyalty to the King independently of the Earl. The most important of those submissions was that of the Bishop of Meath, who had preached the sermon at Lambert Simnel's coronation. His oath of loyalty must have been a
personal triumph for Edgecombe and this is shown in the text.

Ritual Symbolism

Ceremonies, rituals and public displays

The journal is packed with examples of ritual symbolism and public display of authority, ranging from Kildare's intimidating appearance with an escort of 200 horsemen to the spectacular oath-taking ceremony in St Thomas' Monastery. Terms heavy with religious symbolism – such as 'Shriven', 'Agnus', 'Host', 'Altar', 'Te Deum' – are used while the ceremony is described in detail, including a choir singing and bells ringing. By making the ceremony so solemn and public, Edgecombe aimed at ensuring that the Anglo-Irish lords would not renege on their oaths as this would endanger their souls. It is possible that the text puts so much emphasis on these events to cover Edgecombe's failure to secure the lords' submission on the original terms. Later on, Edgecombe put the collar of the King's Livery around Kildare's neck, which the latter wore as he travelled through Dublin. From Edgecombe's perspective this was the ultimate display that royal power vested in him as the King's envoy had triumphed over any form of dissent. On the other hand, Kildare would have accepted this because his oath of allegiance meant he was able to keep his lands and his position as the Lord Deputy of Ireland.

Locations

Locations are also an important element of the symbolism conveyed in the text. The oath ceremony took place in St Thomas' Monastery, which had been founded by King Henry II - again a reference to royal authority. Edgecombe had the Bishop of Meath read out the Pope's Bull of accursing in Christchurch, the location where Lambert Simnel had been crowned. In the other towns he visited, his meetings took place in the Guild Halls, which were the symbolic locations of a city's wealth and power. Last but not least, the locations of the meetings between Edgecombe and Kildare reflect the balance of power between them. Kildare did not meet Edgecombe in Dublin where the latter was lodged, contrary to what would be expected. Instead, he had him come to a place of his choice and only after the oath-taking ceremony was completed, he went to Edgecombe's lodgings. The text does not reveal the reason behind this behaviour, but we can infer that it was part of Kildare's tactics to demonstrate his superiority of rank over Edgecombe, despite the latter representing royal authority.

Conclusion

The source gives us an interesting insight into how communication, rituals and symbols were used by each party as if in a theatrical performance to achieve their objectives and demonstrate their power and authority. However, it also has its limitations. For example, it does not specify what the main sanction would be for the Anglo-Irish lords if they violated the terms of their bond. In addition, the document is a one-sided account of the events, written to justify Sir Richard Edgecombe's actions, and therefore it does not explain Kildare's motivation or the rationale behind his actions. These need to be discovered by the historian in combination with other sources of the time. Nevertheless, 'The Voyage' deserves more attention and analysis by the scholars, which would go beyond its simple use as a means to reconstruct a narrative sequence of events.

Bibliography

Primary Source

'The Voyage of Sir Richard Edgecomb, into Ireland, in the year 1488' in W. Harris (ed), Hibernica Or, Some Antient Pieces Relating to Ireland (Bride Street, 1757), pp. 29-38
The journal can also be accessed online here:
https://celt.ucc.ie/published/E480001-001/index.html

Secondary Works

Bennett, M., Lambert Simnel and the Battle of Stoke (Stroud & New York, 1987)
Bryan, D., Gerald Fitzgerald: The Great Earl of Kildare (1456-1513) (Dublin & Cork, 1933)
Cosgrove, A., Late Medieval Ireland 1370-1541 (Dublin, 1981)
Dumolyn, J., 'Political Communication and Political Power in the Middle Ages: A Conceptual Journey' in Edad Media, Rev. Hist., 13 (2012), pp. 33 – 55
Ellis, S.G., Ireland in the Age of the Tudors 1447-1603: English Expansion and the End of Gaelic Rule (London & New York, 1995)
Ellis, S.G., 'The Great Earl of Kildare (1456-1513) and the Creation of the English Pale' in P. Crooks and S. Duffy (eds), The Geraldines and Medieval Ireland: The Making of a Myth (Dublin, 2016), pp. 325 - 340

Above: The Flat and Police position: Number 22B is the second floor flat on the left. The one on the right is where Imbert and Neville set up their negotiators spot

Right: John Purnell and Author, Steve Moysey

John Purnell GM was the officer that chased the ASU on foot. The picture is on Balcombe Street outside the pub where he ran in to ask the landlord to call 999...

THE IRA REIGN OF TERROR

STEVEN P. MOYSEY

On March 8th, 1973, two car bombs exploded in the center of London, one outside the Old Bailey central criminal court, the other in the street outside a Whitehall building that contained both an army recruiting station and the Ministry of Agriculture. One man was killed and a total of 215 others were wounded in the attacks. Fortunately, two other devices were successfully discovered and defused by the police. This event would mark a shift in the tactics of the Provisional Irish Republican Army (PIRA) in their efforts to pressure for the removal of British forces from Northern Ireland and seek reunification, and self-determination, for the Irish nation. As Belfast Brigade commander Gerry Adams had declared at the time, one bomb in London was worth 20 in Belfast.

The campaign of violence – the bloodiest seen in the UK since the end of WWII – would culminate with the capture of four members of an IRA Active Service Unit (ASU) in December of 1975, after a six-day armed standoff with the police. The four men, in order to avoid capture, had forced their way into the apartment of John and Shelia Mathews on a Saturday evening, as the couple had settled down to watch an episode of the popular police drama "Kojak." Mr. Mathews had mistaken the sound of gunfire from the streets outside as being from the TV show. The flat was in a quiet backstreet only a short walk from London's bustling Marylebone railway station: Balcombe Street. While some may recall the events of the siege, widely covered in the news media at the time, few will recall the deadly buildup that led to the tense armed standoff between the IRA and the Metropolitan Police that cold December week.

While the IRA had targeted mainland Britain since the car bombs of 1973, which they did with murderous efficiency in attacking Birmingham and the Midlands, London was the prime target. The British

Above: Steven P. Moysey, author of "The Road to Balcombe Street"

people had grown somewhat inured to the scenes of bloodshed and destruction in Northern Ireland that beamed into their living rooms each evening on the nightly news. The violence, while dreadful, was across the Irish Sea and many on the mainland viewed the ongoing conflict with a detachment largely born of indifference. The multiple car bomb attacks of March 8th violently shook that indifference, which would be increasingly leveraged by the IRA with string of bombings that further shocked and outraged the nation. However London, as the political, cultural and psychological center of the nation, was the prize the IRA leadership coveted the most and they went after that prize with a bloody focus that would further horrify and outrage the nation. The London ASU's campaign started in earnest on the evening of October 5th, 1974, in an event which would forever change the landscape of terrorism and criminal justice in the UK.

It was on this Saturday evening that the ASU, sent to cause mayhem and destruction to the capital, hit two busy pubs at the peak of their evening trade in the Surrey town of Guildford, twenty-seven miles south of the capital. The timebomb in the Horse and Groom detonated at 8:30 pm, killing a civilian, two members of the Scots Guards and two members of the Women's Royal Army Corps. The nearby Seven Stars was evacuated after the first blast, with the second bomb exploding at 9:00 pm while the pub landlord and his wife searched the premises, injuring the landlord in the process.

The six-man ASU that had blatantly targeted off duty soldiers in Guildford, with no apparent regard for the civilian casualties, struck again with attacks on servicemen's clubs in London, plus a bomb at the famed Harrow public school. But a month after Guildford, they switched back to another pub, only this time with a shrapnel-laden bomb thrown through a window into the Kings Arms in Woolwich, on November 7th. Two people were killed in the explosion and a further 35 people, including the publican, were injured. In a callous example of their murderous calculus, the ASU team had aborted an attack from the preceding evening due to a lack of patrons in the premises.

The London ASU, which later became known as the Balcombe Street ASU, continued their campaign of bombings and shootings, with a short break for a cease fire, largely unimpeded by the police who were at risk of being overwhelmed with the sheer volume of the IRA team's attacks. However, a tragic event would give the police a much-needed break in their investigation. A team of four plain clothes officers were investigating a string of local burglaries when one spotted a "suspicious" individual loitering around outside number 39 Fairholm Road, in W1. On being questioned, the suspect, one Liam Joseph Quinn, a member of the London ASU, fled the scene and triggered a foot chase. The officers were joined in the pursuit of Quinn by 21-year-old off duty police constable Stephen Tibble, who Quinn shot dead in order to secure his escape. A subsequent search of the premise at number 39 revealed a large cache of arms, explosives and intelligence on the London ASU's activities.

The ASU were eventually cornered, in a carefully planned and executed dragnet called Operation Combo, after a repeat attack on West End restaurant. The resulting pursuit and encirclement of the four men in the flat at number 22B Balcombe Street, on December 6th, 1975, is almost the stuff of Hollywood movies, which subsequently earned several members of The Metropolitan Police high medals of bravery in their efforts to capture the IRA men that night. Many of the officers involved in that evening of high drama were only too happy to recall their stories, first hand, to the author. In fact, one officer, retired Deputy Assistant Commissioner John Purnell, an inspector at the time, retraced his steps that night that involved a taxicab, dodging police and IRA terrorist bullets, and a foot chase down a dark alley, in person with the author.

So why is the book, The Road to Balcombe Street, relevant in its telling of events that are close to 50 years ago? It is relevant for several reasons. Firstly, it chronicles the almost Sisyphean efforts of the men

Taunton palace steps: After avoiding both friendly fire and the IRA bullets, Purnell chased the group down the steps from Taunton place to Balcombe street.

and women of the Metropolitan police in their pains to stop a bloody campaign of political inspired terrorism in and around the nation's capital. It also chronicles the multiple bombings, shootings and assassinations conducted by the ASU, and the political elements that led to the IRA camping on the mainland. However, and some may argue more importantly, it highlights a series of events that are still deep scars on the British psyche. After their arrest, the four members of the ASU had readily admitted to and confessed to the facts that they had carried out the Guildford and Woolwich bombings. In fact, during and after their trial and convictions for terrorist offences that did not include Guildford and Woolwich, their leader, Joe O'Connell had freely and publicly admitted to their guilt.

This fact has to be put into the correct context, as Surrey and the Metropolitan Police forces had arrested and convicted two groups of people for the Guildford and Woolwich bombings before the arrest of the Balcombe ASU. As it would later be shown, these were not the only cases that turned out to be wrongful arrests and miscarriages of justice in the IRA terror campaigns that attacked the British mainland during the 1973 – 1975 time period. The Guildford Four, The Maguire Seven, The Birmingham Six, and Judith Ward: all later freed from lengthy prison sentences and exonerated for crimes they did not commit after multiple appeals, hearings, and inquests made it abundantly clear they were innocent. In some cases, their "confessions" had been forcibly obtained by the police using dubious interrogation methods.

As recently as January 2023, The Home Office were still refusing to release key documentation that would help shed much needed light on what was, in hindsight, a much broader and coordinated campaign by the IRA on the British mainland than covered in the book. These same documents could also shine a light on what could be both police and judicial wrongdoing on a systemic basis that have been hidden from public view for these past 50 years.

However, there are still groups of people that find these events more than relevant in their daily lives. These are the families of the murdered and the survivors of the violence that shattered their lives in an instant on evenings in pubs and clubs where they innocently gathered with friends to enjoy what, for some, would be their last. Given the self- confessed roles the ASU had played in two of these key events, and the miscarriages of justice that occurred on multiple fronts, justice and closure for these families is long overdue.

sky cinema

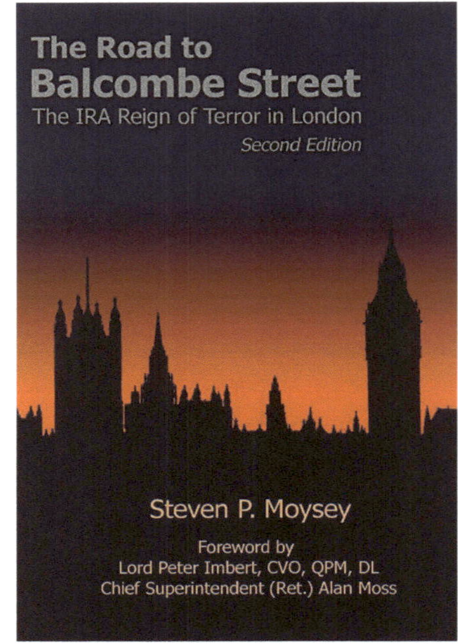

Based on the heart-pounding book "The Road to Balcombe Street" by Steven P. Moysey

Sky Cinema's 2023 movie release of "Dead Shot" on May 15th in the UK - When a border ambush goes wrong, a retired Irish paramilitary Michael (Morgan) witnesses the fatal shooting of his pregnant wife by an SAS officer Tempest (Ameen). After outwitting the SAS, now wounded, and presumed dead, he escapes, taking his revenge to the dark and paranoid streets of 1970's London. Raw and suspenseful, "Dead Shot" is an adrenaline-fueled thriller that will leave audiences weighing up the true cost of revenge.

Starring Aml Ameen, Colin Morgan, Sophia Brown with Mark Strong and Felicity Jones

Learn the art of embroidery, cross-stich,
or tapestry - an art which has endured
throughout history - with these
delightful designs from Bothy Threads!

Bothy Threads Ltd
Unit 7, Aspatria Business Park,
Park Road, Aspatria, Wigton,
Cumbria CA7 3DP, UK

+44 (0)1900 828844
info@bothythreads.com

Elaborately embroidered clothing, religious objects, and household items often were seen as a mark of wealth and status, as in the case of Opus Anglicanum, a technique used by professional workshops and guilds in medieval England.[6] In 18th-century England and its colonies, samplers employing fine silks were produced by the daughters of wealthy families. Embroidery was a skill marking a girl's path into womanhood as well as conveying rank and social standing. - Wikipedia

Henry Arthur Payne (1868–1940) "Plucking the Red and White Roses in the Old Temple Gardens"
This is the preliminary painting for a mural in the East Corridor of the Palace of Westminster, - Wikimedia

PLATINUM SPONSORS

Helena P. Schrader

Susanne Dunlap

SILVER SPONSORS

BOOKOUTURE

Tess Thompson

THE HISTORICAL FICTION COMPANY BOOK OF THE YEAR 2022

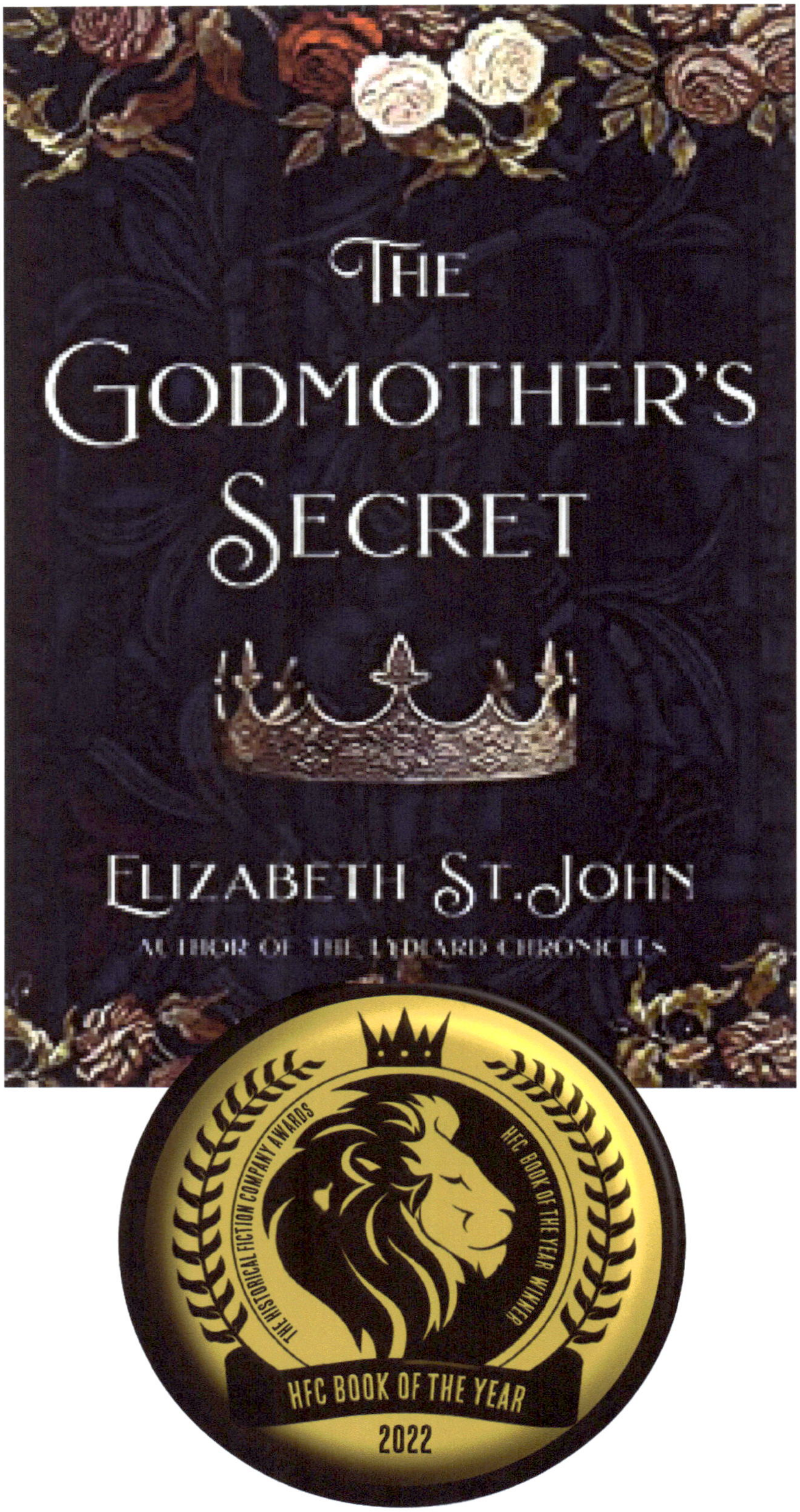

Elizabeth St. John
Historical Fiction Author

Elizabeth St. John's critically acclaimed historical fiction novels tell the stories of her ancestors: extraordinary women whose intriguing kinship with England's kings and queens brings an intimately unique perspective to Medieval, Tudor, and Stuart times.

Inspired by family archives and residences from Lydiard Park to the Tower of London, Elizabeth spends much of her time exploring ancestral portraits, diaries, and lost gardens. And encountering the occasional ghost. But that's another story.

Living between California, England, and the past, Elizabeth is the International Ambassador for The Friends of Lydiard Park, an English charity dedicated to conserving and enhancing this beautiful centuries-old country house and park. As a curator for The Lydiard Archives, she is constantly looking for an undiscovered treasure to inspire her next novel.

Elizabeth's books include her trilogy, The Lydiard Chronicles, set in 17th Century England during the Civil War, and her newest release, The Godmother's Secret, which explores the medieval mystery of the missing Princes in the Tower of London.

The Godmother's Secret by Elizabeth St. John

The truth of my appointment yawns like a gorge between us; the men may fight across hill and dale, but the women draw their own York and Lancaster battle lines across planked and herb-strewn chamber floors.

Many, many stories and speculations have bloomed throughout the centuries about the fate of the famous princes of the Tower – Edward and Richard, or affectionately known as Ned and Dickon – the two little boys who disappeared one night from the Tower of London, one as heir to the throne of England and the other as a Duke of York. Offspring of Edward IV and Elizabeth Woodville, the two boys stood in the way of others seeking the throne, such as Richard of Gloucester, Edward IV's brother, and Henry Tudor, the son of Margaret Beaufort. As stated, many stories have been told of this event, all with their own slant, but this one is presented with such finesse and skill, with such clarity and authenticity, as to sway a mind and heart in a way that a work of artistic literature should do. This fictional account of what possibly happened is so moving and so well-developed, a reader might close the book on the speculations and say, in effect, "This is it; this is what happened. No doubt."

These wars. These wars that men fight and women endure, waiting for news, for their men to return home - - or not. This new prince, born into conflict, swaddled by dispute, and nursed with vengeance. This wheel of destiny as old as mankind. No one questions if it can be halted. At least no man does. And the women walk behind God's chari-

ot of war as they always have and salvage the wreckage.

To summarize this astounding work, as this reviewer will strive to do, does not even render the force with which Ms. St. John gifts this story to us. And it is a gift, a splendid gift of pure cerebral enjoyment, the epitome of what a historical fiction book should be.

We come to know on a very intimate level the character of Elysabeth St. John, Lady Scrope (and the author's ancestress), who becomes the godmother to a king-in-waiting the night she assists Elizabeth Woodville, the Queen of England and wife of Edward IV, in childbirth. The Queen gives birth to her son, Edward (Ned), and Lady Scrope makes a vow to protect the boy from harm for the rest of her life. As the author states in her notes at the end of the book, who better to know what exactly happened to the boys than their godmother who was with them for the majority of their life? Thus, the story follows Lady Scrope as she maneuvers and protects the boys from the day of their birth, until the day Edward IV dies and his son is taken to the Tower by his uncle, Richard of Gloucester, to prepare for the boy's coronation. In short order, his brother, Richard (Dickon) joins him there.

Sovereynté, King Arthur's tales tell me, is what women desire the most. The power to make our own decisions. Freedom from control. More than love, more than friendship, we desire power. And when the power of sovereynté was given to me in the form of an urgent appeal and a pearl crucifix, I grabbed it with both hands. Just three weeks ago, I was at home by the hearth, the woman's natural place, my life spinning before me in the predictable warp and weft of family and friends. Today, because of my sovereynté, I am

riding with the King of England to prepare for his coronation.

Yet, behind the scenes of the political chaos brewing, you truly come to know this woman who is as loyal as anyone might be in these trying times. A very poignant scene where there is a discussion about choices of mottos, when the young Edward decides his motto ("God and My Right") and his uncle, Richard, quotes his motto, Loyaltié me lie (loyalty binds me), where you get a sense of Lady Scrope's own mind, and how her sovereignty, her right to make decisions as a woman, plays out in this story, which sometimes puts her at odds with her own husband and with her half-sister, Margaret Beaufort. While Lady Scrope thinks only of the boy's safety and happiness, others seek their own advantage. Margaret seeks the throne for her son, Henry Tudor, who is in France and looking for an opportunity to seize the throne as the true heir; and Richard, Edward IV's brother, who takes the throne after Edward IV's marriage to Elizabeth Woodville is declared as invalid, thus rendering the children bastards.

"Remember the inn, when you told us what women want?"

"Sovereynté," I say.

"Yes," he replies. "The power to make their own decisions." The king pauses as we approach the castle walls, flexes his shoulders as if they ache.

"You are left behind to be in charge reynté. You are tasked with the most important power of all. Keeping the boys alive and sending them safely to their next destination. Wait for Catesby's instructions. Enlist Oliver's help. And, most of all, remember my words. Remember the stalking horse."

Again and again, Lady Scrope tries to check on the

Editorial Reviews

boys while they are in the tower, worrying as Edward falls sick, and herself falling into different schemes conjured by Margaret and the Duke of Buckingham. Time after time, she comes close to very traitorous situations, yet with her husband, a faithful and loyal defender of King Richard, and showing her own loyalty by upholding her vow, she is witness to and, ultimately, a party to the eventual outcome for the two boys... a quite unexpected and different outcome as revealed in accepted history. And not only that, but you are privy to the inner heart and mind of a woman very close to all of these historical events and people, as well as how it might have felt for a woman facing loss, love, betrayal, fear, and anxiety while showing incredible strength, loyalty, determination, and courage while those around her fought for the hollow crown. Not much is actually known about Lady Scrope, but with this tale being told by a descendant, Elizabeth St. John, the author, the authenticity and historical research displayed within this story is immense and exquisite. Ms. St. John is sure to be a new found favorite for fans of not only this fractious time in English history, but of all historical fans who adore rich, immersive prose.

"The Godmother's Secret" by Elizabeth St. John receives five stars and the "Highly Recommended" award of excellence by The Historical Fiction Company

*　*　*　*　*

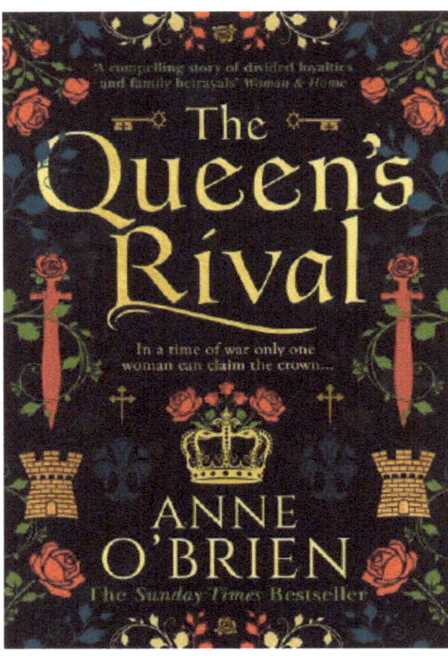

**THE QUEEN'S RIVAL
by Anne O'Brien**

First and foremost, I applaud Anne O'Brien for tackling this topic, that of the War of the Roses, from the unique viewpoint of Cecily Neville, the Duchess of York, and I give her even more credit for presenting this book in the format that she chose. I must say, I have never read a historical novel done in this way and I was astounded at the perfection in which we are offered an insight into the minds of so many involved in this history. To be honest, I wasn't sure at first that I was going to like reading letter entries from one character to another, a story being told this way, but after the first few, I was hooked. I think this is a remarkable way to get into a character's mind, after all, what can be more intimate than a letter from one person to another. And then, with the smattering of news reports from the England's Chronicle to round out the storyline and the personal messages of recipes betwixt sisters (Cecily, Anne, and Katharine), well, I think this was genius. The story starts from the Duke of York's rebellion against Henry VI, and his fleeing to Ireland, leaving his wife, Cecily,

and their three youngest children at Ludlow Castle to face the forces of Lancaster. All told in letter form as she writes to her sisters, Anne, Duchess of Buckingham, and Katherine, Dowager Duchess of Norfolk, as well as other letters dispersed throughout between many other characters (Marguerite, Queen of England; Richard, Duke of York; etc.) From that development, we learn a great deal about Cecily's mind set as she maneuvers her children, her sons, in an attempt to bring her husband's wishes about in securing the throne of England under their rightful Yorkist claim. Through this intimate way of communication, you truly delve deep into hearts and minds, and feel the passion of Cecily, not only for the royal blood she possesses but her love for her husband and her children, as well as her passionate dislikes. I think the only thing that confused me a bit about the book is the title – "The Queen's Rival" – Although I understood, I suppose, that Cecily was the rival of Queen Marguerite, and then eventually, in some respect, the rival as Queen Mother to her son's wife after he became King; however, the title did not imbue, to me, what the story was truly about, that is, this brave and strong woman, Cecily, Duchess of York. Again, perhaps it was just my thoughts but that being said, the title did not at all distract from the brilliance of the story. I loved the depth and incredible research and the daring approach that Anne O'Brien took in retelling this tale in a very unique form. I highly recommend this book and give it five stars!!

*　*　*　*　*

SENLAC: BOOK ONE
by Julian De La Motte

Senlac opens during Christmas of the year 1065, a time of grave national crisis and disquieting omens, when the aged King Edward the Confessor, the seventh son of Æthelred the Unready, dies in the Palace of Westminster in London. He leaves behind no heir. To fill the void, Edward's brother-in-law, Harold, the Earl of Wessex, the greatest warrior in England, is hurriedly elected king by popular acclaim. Harold desperately seeks to unify a kingdom ravaged by the Danish occupation, and by unrest on both the Scottish and Welsh borders. To ensure military support in the north, Harold must turn his back on his beloved common-law wife, Edith the Fair—also known as Edith Swanneck, for the graceful length of her neck—and their children, to marry Aeldyth, the sister of both the Earl of Northumbria and the Earl of Mercia. Meanwhile, Harold's mercurial younger brother, Tostig, is bitterly plotting a return from exile and revenge against the King. Across the North Sea, the King of Norway, the aging and psychotic Harald Hardraada, who was said to be a full

seven feet tall, dreams of a new Viking Empire on English soil, and strikes an alliance with Tostig. Likewise, across the English Channel, William, Duke of Normandy—the leader of a powerful yet unstable military state—plans his own attack, determined to avenge Harold's broken promise to make England his. After all, Edward the Confessor swore to make William his heir and he is determined to take what is rightfully his.

To say this book is a lustrous epic is putting it mildly; and not only does the author present us with one book spanning the years of the Norman Conquest, but we have two illustrious books which stand alongside classics such as Les Miserables, and War and Peace. To get the full sense and understanding of the time period, and of William's claim and conquest, one MUST read both books, and believe me, you won't regret the time you spend immersing yourself in this era of English history. From the very beginning, the entire scene depicting Edward the Confessor's death, the urging of those around him to name an heir, to the incredible clarity the author has to the details in the room, you might mistake this book for a non-fiction book relaying a detailed rendering from an actual eyewitness; as if Mr De La Motte stood in the room and wrote down each and every movement, smell, sight, noise, color, and whisper in full rich expostulation. But what he does is offer the reader a glorious retelling weaving facts with fiction in a way that you cannot tell which is which – the skill of a masterful bard. Oftentimes, readers are intimidated by the presentation of a list of characters at the beginning of a book – long lists of everyone involved in the history – and might feel overwhelmed to sort out who is who as the narrative devel-

ops, but the author's skill at introducing characters and fleshing them out is a work of art. From the first introduction of William, Duke of Normandy, you are given incredible insight to him as a person, again as if the author traveled back in time and dictated all that he saw. I knew a little about William from my own historical research and interest in this time period, but not nearly the extent to which Mr De La Motte delves; and yet, with the amount of narrative versus dialogue you might think this novel to be heavy, but it is not, it is beautifully written in a way that moves a reader along the journey instead of bogging down in overt historical detail.

Other authors I think of is the richness of Edward Rutherford and the deep layers of Hilary Mantel's books, and those who enjoy their books will definitely enjoy these two. Upon the death of Edward, Harold, the Earl of Wessex, is made King of England, and the echoes of this occurrence reverberates across the Channel to the other claimants of the throne – William, Duke of Normandy, and Harald Hadraada, King of Norway – all with their own supposed promises from Edward the Confessor. And then you have Tostig, the quicksilver brother of King Harold, who has his own agenda against his brother and his sights set on Northumbria. He imagines with a little coin in his pocket, a few ships, and promising alliance with one of the contenders for the throne will secure his ultimate **gain, and his first try is upon William**. But William is clever, which stands out with skill in this book, and is always the preeminent chess-player in the world of medieval politics and maneuvering to bring about his goal. I loved the line about Tostig –

Editorial Reviews

"Between them, Baldwin and William will vie with each other to get as much from him as possible whilst giving him as little as possible."

So much trouble brewing from all angles around the island of England as Harold tries to sort out where his support will come from. Tostig even has good rapport with the Scots; storms are surging in Ireland and Wales; no one to stand with him from Mercia and Northumbria – Harold is between a rock and a hard place, not to mention his recurring nightmare of the chalk giant of Cernas Abbas (of which I will not give away!). After reading these two books there is no doubt in your mind of the fierce and determined historical personages of this era and the actions they take; plus the resolute reasons as to why William becomes known as the Conqueror. I also enjoyed very much getting to know the women behind these men, especially Edith known as 'swan neck' although her husband calls her 'hard head' in private, and felt a deep sympathy for her as she is discarded in favor of a match to Aeldyth (his political bride) that he must make as King since he is only hand-fasted to Edith and not married in the eyes of the church; and yet, she acquiesces to this in a surprising way, as you will see in reading. A very enlightening revelation of the feminine side of politics, the whispers in bed chambers, the meanings behind tapestry-making, and how women were used along this journey of men's ambitions. Another intriguing line which sent shivers up my spine was a visit to his sister, Edie, and she says "Do you want to know the time and manner of your death?"

More ominous omens haunting the air and pounding Harold's brain, or perhaps his own guilt at not fulfilling the oath he swore to William of setting him on England's throne? All of these small details are exquisite tidbits captivating the reader in this story, and ones that I truly found appealing. If I was to relay all the insightful and masterful descriptions of the book, I might be writing another book about a book, for there are so many instances of pure writing genius. My sound advice is to read this one for yourself, for it is a worthy one for you to treasure for years to come; buy the book, read it, keep it on your shelf, for this is one you will want to read again and again, and I suspect each time you will find another little treasure hidden within the words that you overlooked before.

Yes, this book begins the story of William the Conqueror, but also gives us a picture of Mr De La Motte's masterful skill at conquering words and weaving them into an immense beautiful tapestry of 11th-century English history. This is a book every English literature or history professor must have to recreate in their student's minds a depiction of the age for even though it is presented as fiction, the authenticity stands out as factual. For fans of quality, immersive, rich, emotional, believable, classic-worthy, stand-out historical literature, this is it. Five stars from The Historical Fiction Company!

*　*　*　*　*

SENLAC: BOOK TWO
by Julian De La Motte

In Book Two of *Senlac*, the inevitable happens; forces are engaged in violent, bloody war. Each of the three powerful leaders are forced to the very limit of their abilities and resources as they fight to achieve their ambitious goals. The result is the tragic year of The Three Battles, the death of thousands of warriors and common people conscripted for the carnage, and the destruction of a whole way of life. Nothing was ever the same again.

A scourge is let loose on England, in the form of Tostig, one-time Earl of Northumbria and the exiled brother of King Harold of England, joining forces with some of the north men of Alba (King Malcolm Canmore of Scotland, and the fierce King of Norway) all for his own advantage. After opening with an up-to-date account of all that transpired in Book One (which is a clever device for the author to have used to allow this book to be read as a stand-alone which, by the way, I do not recommend – both books need to be devoured and enjoyed), we are taken directly into the action. And when

I say action, this book (as well as book one) is full of meaty action playing in a reader's mind like an epic movie.

Three battles play out in this book, all leading to the culmination upon Senlac Hill between King Harold and William, Duke of Normandy. You think you know the story, as many who are fed on the history of the Battle of Hastings, but to read the details offered in this novel is simply incredible writing.

Harold, crowned King after Edward the Confessor's death, faces three invasions – from his own brother Tostig, the fierce Norwegian King Hardraada, and from William, Duke of Normandy – all with their own agendas and motives against England. Tostig and Hardraada combine forces and defeat some of the English at the Battle of Fulford, but then are defeated by Harold at the Battle of Stamford Bridge. With two opponents down, Harold turns his attention to the taunts of William, and even rejects another offer of a 'Dux Anglorum' position after taking a child bride with a new heir on the way. There was no turning back. He was determined to remain King, or go down fighting. After William lands his invasion force, Harold marches south to meet him, all converging near Hastings at Senlac Hill.

Some of my favorite lines from the book: -Tostig played upon the King of the Scots as he might upon a musical instrument, teasing out appropriate notes at appropriate points.- -It was a season, as a consequence, of food poisoning and collective hallucinogenic mass visions and hysteria brought on by the eating of what the people called 'the crazy bread.' It was a season for outbreaks and violence and visions and the prophesying of the deranged. These crazed unfortu-nates haunted the woods and the fields and the riverbanks. - (Very Shakespearean!!) -"Well, best to get started, I suppose, before we all die of old age," It was a curiously flat and simple statement with which to set such a momentous act in motion.- I loved these two lines, the first spoken by William, with the narrative setting William's mood and final words before a battle which changed history. Just brilliant!

Again, so much praise for this novel that is Shakespearean to the highest degree – with epic battles, era-accurate dialogue, poetic descriptions, and intriguing omen-inspired threads weaving through the story line as if Mr De La Motte held his ear against the Bayeux Tapestry to hear the tale unfold. Even the way the author wraps up the story with what happens to the main women in the story is perfection – Edith (Harold's hand-fasted wife), Gytha, his mother, and Aeldyth, his Queen – all their real stories fade into history, but here we are offered a view into what might have happened to them after the Battle of Hastings, and the offering is very believable.

This is truly the Bayeux Tapestry come to life! Mr De La Motte gives writers an exquisite lesson on how to write a historical novel, and he gives readers a glorious future classic to enjoy. This book is lush, atmospheric, and worthy of the highest praise.

Five stars from The Historical Fiction Company!!

* * * * *

ALL MANNER OF THINGS
by Wendy J. Dunn

Winter, 1539: María de Salinas is dying. Too ill to travel, she writes a letter to her daughter Katherine, the young duchess of Suffolk. A letter telling of her life: a life intertwined with her friend and cousin Catalina of Aragon, the youngest child of Isabel of Castile. It is a letter to help her daughter understand the choices she has made in her life, beginning from the time she keeps her vow to Catalina to share her life of exile in England. Friendship. Betrayal. Hatred. Forgiveness. Love wins out in the end.

The year is 1501 and a retinue of retainers and attendants is accompanying the royal daughter of Spain, Catalina of Aragon, from Spain to England where she will meet and wed the heir to the English throne, the young Prince Arthur Tudor, son of Henry VII. Among her attendants is her dearest friend María de Salinas, who brings with her a love of music and poetry and a rich knowledge of herbalism and healing. Maria and Catalina are all of fifteen years old at this point, just past childhood, but nonetheless pawns in the great chess

Editorial Reviews

match of alliances and pacts between the great powers of sixteenth-century Europe.

All Manner of Things is the second book in the series Falling Pomegranate Seeds, which traces the life of Catalina of Aragon, youngest daughter of King Ferdinand of Aragon and Queen Isabella of Castile.

The story is told through María's eyes as, towards the end of her life, she pens a letter to her daughter. Through her recollections, her own letters to her tutor back in Spain, poetry, and a selection of texts from the period, we accompany her through the years. It is her own story that she tells to her daughter, but it is not only her story, for as one of Catalina's noble serving women, Maria's story is inextricably entwined with that of the princess.

Thus it is that the reader joins the royal retinue, moving from those first days of separation from family and everything they know, to England's cold and foreign shores, to life under the protection – or is that imprisonment? – of Henry Tudor. Maria stays with her dear friend during a short and heartbreaking half-marriage with gentle Prince Arthur, and through a tumultuous second marriage to the young and brash new king of England, Henry VIII, when she becomes known to her people as Queen Katherine, and to the history books as Katherine of Aragon.

Author Wendy J. Dunn paints an exquisitely detailed picture of the English court at the time. She brings us into the castles and courts of the kings where we meet stern and forbidding Henry Tudor and his compassionate wife. We celebrate the growing affection between Catalina and Arthur and grieve with the princess at her royal husband's death. And then, through years of spiteful neglect, we struggle

with the Spanish contingent as they exist in a strained limbo, Catalina being neither wife nor widow, playthings to the men of power as they work their machinations of politics.

Likewise, we are witness to the casual brutality and violence of Henry VIII's regime once he takes power, and cry with the new queen with each lost baby as she watches her new husband's affection ebb in his quest for passion and an heir. And all around, the politics swirls, touching the edges of the narrative with its relentlessness, casting the powerlessness of the women into sharp relief.

This, Dr. Dunn accomplishes with a deft hand. Under the guidance of her pen, the men and women from our history books take on real life. Through meticulous research and skilled characterization, they become flesh and blood, cruel and kind, selfish and loving, and very real. She also takes the convoluted political manoeuvrings of the early sixteenth century and frames them in a context that renders them immediate and comprehensible. All those alliances and pacts and agreements that cover the pages of our textbooks are made real on the pages of her book. These actors are not an assortment of names and titles, but they are Catalina's kin. And as Catalina discovers her place in this world of shifting alliances, so too does María come to terms with her own fate, and that of her family.

While the narrative arc of *All Manner of Things* is as carefully constructed as any novel, the main events are true and the characters were real people. Catalina, of course, was Henry VIII's first wife, and María was indeed one of her attendants. And as Catalina grows from timid and superstitious girl into a woman fit to

be Queen of England, so does María grow. Her final act of love towards her friend – no spoilers – shows how strong her difficult life made her. This, too, was a real event. María, it seems, might have been a pawn in the hands of the powerful men around her, but she was not one to just give up, and we love her more for it.

My quibbles about this book are few and far between. It was, perhaps, a bit slow at the beginning, and I would have liked to know more about María's life after her marriage, although that was not the focus of the story. There were also one or two small threads of narrative that were left unresolved, tensions raised and then abandoned. But these were very minor issues, more of a wish-list than a litany of complaints.

In sum, I can think of almost nothing I would change about this book. It is beautifully written with realistic and sympathetic characters, and shot through with the golden threads of music and poetry that bring the era to full life. If Tudor history is your passion – or even if it's not – this is a book to enjoy again and again.

Five Stars from The Historical Fiction Company, "Highly Recommended" Award

*   *   *   *   *

THE RIPPON SPURRIER
by C. J. Richardson

"By Jesu, Robert. You are an excellent spurrier and silver-smith," said Richard. "I have not seen this quality of workmanship outside of London. You will make Rippon famous." He turned to Thomas, adding, "And you, my nephew, will wear spurs charged with Catholic spirit when we ride out. We cannot fail in our noble task now."

Talented spurrier Robert Gray has always admired his late father Alfred for taking part in the Pilgrimage of Grace many years ago, so he jumps at the chance to march alongside his own master in a rebellion against the heretic Queen Elizabeth in the autumn of 1569. As a staunch Catholic, taking part in this holy war would be a dream come true. He did not expect that dream would put his wife Catherine and their unborn child in mortal danger.

This novel is proof that there is never enough books about the Tudor era, and a plethora of hidden characters waiting to be revealed on the page. As the rebellion begins in Northeast England against Queen Elizabeth the First with the goal of re-establishing the Catholic faith and placing Mary, Queen of Scots, on the throne, a talented spurrier, Robert Grey, joins the cause. Both he and his wife, Catherine, are faithful Catholics, swearing loyalty to support the faith even at the risk of their own lives. Following in the footsteps of his own father who fought against Henry VIII's break from Rome, Robert's determination brings his wife, his unborn child, and himself close to danger as the threats mount.

The story unfolds, and betrayal surfaces when Robert's lifelong friend turns against him; and secrets of the past involving his father's death bubble to the surface causing great distress and many a sleepless night for Robert. Yet, even in this, he is determined to reveal all, even as the one person in opposition to him shows the same determination to keep them hidden.

In a fight for survival of their family, of friendships, and of honour, Robert and Catherine bind together to ensure their very lives... and all as the repercussions of Henry's rejection of the Catholic church come full force upon nobleman and commoner, alike.

Robert, like the majority of English Catholics of 1569, supported Mary's claim to the throne and viewed her as a way to restore the faith to England. In Northern England, several powerful nobles such as Charles Neville, 6th Earl of Westmorland, and Thomas Percy, 7th Earl of Northumberland, held fast to their Catholic faith and vowed an uprising against Queen Elizabeth. Robert joins in the rebellion, the same as his father before him had joined in the Pilgrimage of Grace against Henry VIII in 1536. Mary became their beacon of hope against the heretic.

There is so much vivid detail in this book that you are immediately drawn into the past, reliving a time when loyalty is tested and 'windows' are made into men's souls – Catholic against Protestant, and vice versa. With each decision made or side chosen, the shadows lurk ready to betray those who hold fast to their Catholic leanings, those hiding their rosaries in secret places and holding mass with whispers.

Yet, Robert and Catherine's love and strength, supporting each other through this time as they stand united in their convictions, is a nod to the beauty and courage of unshakeable faith, even with the heat of betrayal breathing down their neck.

Without giving anything away, I must say that the world-building and the author's gift of story-telling is astounding and transports the reader to the stage of sixteenth century England and Scotland with very believable characters and natural dialogue befitting the time period. So meticulously researched and words chosen with finesse to create this story of their lives so as to immerse the reader in a world which, even though we know what happens from history, we find ourselves rooting for the main characters.

As relayed from the viewpoint of Robert and Catherine, the tragic events of October 1569 to January 1570 unfold. Robert, whose flair for metal work, especially his artistry for forging beautiful spurs in his village of Rippon; and his wife Catherine whose partial blindness does little to hinder her wide view of the events around them, even as she is labelled a witch, see their common life evolve as some of the key figures in the rebellion come into their life – Anne (also pregnant) and Thomas Percy (one of the leaders of the rebellion). Robert's master and patron, Thomas Markenfield, is first to join the conflict and Robert follows him, pledging loyalty and service to the Earls of Northumbria and Westmorland, while Catherine becomes a servant to Anne, Thomas's wife.

While history gives us the larger details of the rebellion, C. J. Richardson focuses the attention on the intimate way such conflicts change people's lives, and she does this in quite a skilful and sensitive way. What begins as excitement and the hopeful prospect of bringing back their former way of life develops from triumph to the ultimate failure of the uprising and the need for Robert to protect his family.

Some of my favourite vivid passages to give an overview of the author's artistry:

"The fog had lifted, and the winter sun tried to deceive us into thinking its rays cast warmth upon us, but its bright face served only to light up the ice on the rutted road and the newly formed icicles hanging from the boughs of the trees... She saw only the beauty of the landscape instead of feeling the bitter bite of the air around us. I knew it was because she was thinking about home in Rippon."

"There was a commotion outside. I could hear screaming and shouting. I got up and went to the window. The crowds were thick. Soldiers. Mary, Mother of God. The soldiers were rounding up men by the score and tying their hands together, using a rope to join them like a string of onions, then marching them to the obelisk on the market stede.... I looked down on the helmet of a soldier who had a taut rope fastened to his saddle, a limp body trailing through the dirty street behind him."

Vivid imagery worthy of the "Highly Recommended" award from The Historical Fiction Company and five stars!! Congratulations to the author for this fine work of art of the Tudor era.

*   *   *   *   *

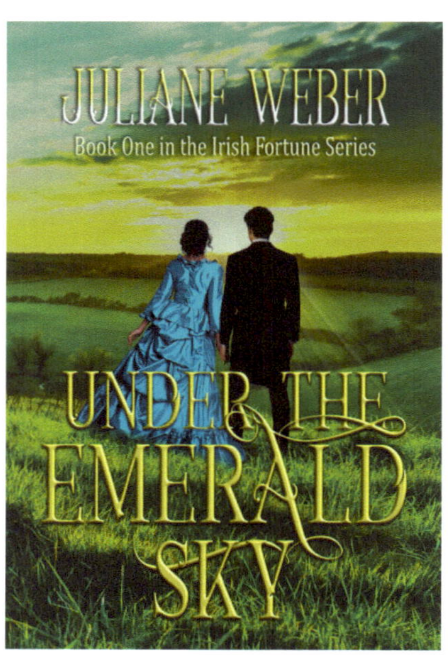

**UNDER THE EMERALD SKY
by Juliane Weber**

Although this was an occupation that I would otherwise have enjoyed, doing nothing else left me feeling empty, unfulfilled, like a beautiful vase stashed away at the back of the cupboard, gathering dust.

"Quinton Fletcher Philbert Williams, at your service, ma'am," he declared and bowed. "My parents felt it necessary to burden me with the greatest number of dreadful names they could come up with."

And thus we are introduced to the two captivating main characters in the book, and from the first line to the last line, this is a book which excites and intrigues in the way a classic Historical Romance novel should do. This is a romance for the ages, and one I could not put down until I absorbed

each and every event in Quinton and Alannah's life.

Quinton, a very English gentleman (and devastatingly handsome to boot), comes to Ireland to oversee and restore his father's holdings at the failing estate of Glaslearg. Many Englishmen held estates in Ireland, leaving the running to overseers and raking in the cash brought in by tenants while never stepping foot onto their properties, thus submitting many of the poor oppressed by heavy fees and very little sustenance. Quinton comes to Glaslearg as quite the different sort of Englishman, one who sees the suffering and wants to correct the ills wrought upon those in the estate's care. One problem – he cannot speak Gaelic, and his tenants cannot speak English. Second problem – many of the Irish despise the English and are seeking a way to oust them from their island by any means necessary. Third problem – he is running from a past which shows up later in the story.

Alannah O'Neill, a beautiful strong-willed dark-haired Irish woman whose father doted on her, providing her with an education and bolstering her ambitions, succumbs to the oppressive hand of her brother, Kieran, after her father suddenly dies and leaves the farm to his son, and Alannah without a say in her future.

Kieran's opinions about women were hardly unique, of course – in a male-dominated society that masqueraded behind superficial chivalry, prejudiced beliefs about women's naivete and their excessive sensitivity were easily excused, if not actively encouraged. While many men genuinely seemed to love their female relations, a good number of these same men nevertheless recoiled at the thought of giving women more freedom.

But after hearing that the neighboring estate owner needs some help with the Gaelic-speaking tenants, she snatches up the opportunity to help out. The magnetism between her and Quin is evident from the start, and Ms Weber does a magical job of drawing the reader into this passionate romance reminiscent of early Victorian classic couples like Darcy and Elizabeth mingling with sexy couples like Jaime Fraser and Clare Randall.

Inevitably, their love grows at a galloping pace, and so does the troubles as Alannah's brother threatens to marry her off to a good Irishman while spouting his disgust for the English. And then, when a dangerous associate of Kieran's comes into the picture, someone whose violent ways and determination to rouse the Irish against the English brings near disaster upon Quinton and Alannah, their future and their love is tested to the fullest extent possible.

There are so many great things to say about this novel – the layers are so perfectly entwined, yet the story opens up like a blossoming rose as Ms Weber takes you by the hand and leads you through the travails of living during this turbulent time in Irish history – a time when the politics of the nobility held sway, where only a smattering of the Irish actually owned their own land, and how so many suffered from lack of decent food and housing. The author immerses the reader into the Irish landscape – you are there, gazing over the emerald fields, rooting for the success of Quinton's efforts, and for this 'forbidden' love between an Englishman and an Irish lass to prevail; not to mention the rich description of how Guinness extra stout tastes on the tongue!

So many places with sublime imagery – such as page 260 where she traces 'the star-shaped scar that marred the right side of his chest, just beneath the collarbone' to the 'long line that snaked its way along the left side of his abdomen... still an angry red.... tracing the line lightly with my index finger.' - Just so exquisite and intimate in such a way that makes these character alive.

Or page 267 where the author relays the politics of landowners and tenants, doing so with such ease and not overburdening the reader with too much – just enough historical fact to add to the narrative, and this is done again and again, effortlessly.

I even loved the added tidbit on page 312 about how long it takes for an author to write a book, or how a 'writer is led. be that to the amusement of some or the disappointment of others...' - to which, I say, this novel is both entertaining and not a single page of disappointment. I know readers wil find a treasure trove of their own favorite passages to reac again and again.

The characters are SO believable, and the emotions, both intimate and public, are incredibly relatable; so much so that Under the Emerald Sky reaches another level in storytelling – the kind where the characters remain with you long after you have closed the book, and you are longing to know what happens next for them. I, for one, cannot wait for the next installment!!

Under the Emerald Sky by Juliane Weber receives five stars and the "Highly Recommended" award from The Historical Fiction Company

*　*　*　*　*

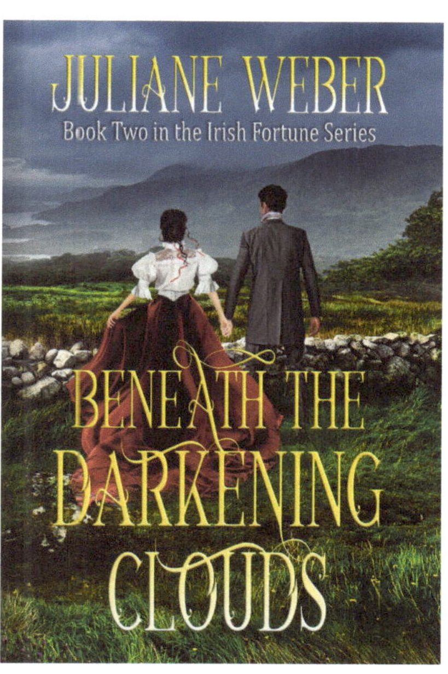

BENEATH THE DARKENING CLOUDS
by Juliane Weber

Historical romance readers can rest assured that Juliane Weber has delivered a very strong second book in the Irish Fortune Series. The story picks up where the last novel ended, with the young Alannah and Quinton now married and settling at Glaslearg to establish a family. Although the journey of this young Anglo-Irish family proves to be challenging, the protagonists, with their strengths, beauty, and justice, are set to endure and prevail.

Juliane Weber's book is a clever mix of love story, suspense, and Gaelic lore, in which Irish history plays an important role. Fans of the genre are rewarded with a sweet romance in which the tension propels them read the book faster.

The story is set in Ireland in the spring of 1845. In 1801 the country was forced into a union with England to create the United Kingdom of Great Britain and Ireland. Here is how Quin, an English landlord determined to make a better life for his Irish tenants, sees the country:

Editorial Reviews

"...centuries of oppression and poor land management by their English conquerors had left Irish commoners with little to call their own, and even less chance of improvement."

From the first line, Weber captivates the reader by offering them a glimpse of the dangers yet to come. Then masterfully, the author let us know that the worries are real even if it was just a dream. The couple had made powerful enemies determined to win at any expense. So, we meet the evil contender Mr. Andrews who will stalk Quin through the story to kill him, revealing his antagonist character. We are compelled to follow Alannah and Quin to see how this will play out while we are introduced to secondary characters and their stories and dramas.

Along, we learn much about Ireland's history and culture, from its Gaelic heritage, such as language and rituals, to its more recent clashes with British aristocracy over exploitation of the country and its inhabitants. Irish festivals where Celtic magic overlaps the strong catholic tradition or Irish attitudes towards English oppression are only a few of the historical references we are presented through the book while the characters navigate their indubitable destiny.

Everything revolves around Alannah and Quin and their growing passion amid their desires to become parents. But the story's conflict doesn't come from the main character's internal struggles. It is not their love that's challenged, but their life. We do not fear for the survival of their love. Still, we dread the dangers from external forces that threaten their physical survival, Quin by the hands of an evil man, Alannah by nature's unleashed malevolence.

The plot unfolds slowly, culminating in the novel's second part like a good story arc should do. No disappointments here. Moreover, while we are led to believe that the danger is gone, another more significant threat is around the corner: the Great Famine and its devastating effects on Ireland.

In the end, the love between Alannah and Quin remains unchallenged and productive, but the immediacy of death is more present than ever, and we will fear for their lives beyond the novel's last words. The main characters are whole, fleshy, and blessed with flawlessness, slightly vanilla in the absence of any vice to stain their perfect personality.

Alannah, the daughter of an Irish gentry man, shows traits unusual for ladies of the early Victorian era: she is smart and had received a good education; she's interested in science, a domain where she can sustain a conversation with men in professional fields. Nevertheless, she is still a woman facing the same obtuse mindsets as any other of her gender. The author expresses the attitudes toward females in the following exchange between Mr. Andrews, the villain, and our protagonist, Quin:

Women, of course," he went on earnestly before Quin had recovered sufficiently from his shock to respond, "can't be expected to understand such things. They are simply too soft...and too irrational. That's why they need a man to keep them in line...and make such choices for them." "Is that so?" Quin growled, eying Andrews with extreme dislike. Andrews, however, paid no attention to Quin whatsoever. "If you ask me," the vile man said, "most women are useful for precisely one thing."

Alannah is not only a woman but an Irish woman who must overcome her father-in-law's hostility, who perhaps had hoped for a different arrangement for his son.

Quin, the son of an English baron with properties in Ireland, defies his family's rigid expectations and quits the British army to become "a farmer," as his father called him, dissatisfied with his only son's choice. Owning an estate in Ireland, he must consider the needs of his servants and tenants, impoverished Irish folks wary of England's aristocracy. By the end of the story, Alannah and Quin will prove worthy of respect from Quin's father and Glaslearg community.

With a skillful pen, Weber portrays the characters and settings with historical accuracy for the era. She is a natural in using the language of the time, and even though it may seem a little magisterial to the modern reader, the way the author narrates and builds dialog is perfectly natural to the characters in mid-nineteen century Ireland. And if there is any anticipatory work to be done, it is the desire that Juliane Weber quickly writes the follow-up.

"Beneath the Darkening Clouds" by Juliane Weber receives five stars from The Historical Fiction Company and the "Highly Recommended" award of excellence.

* * * * *

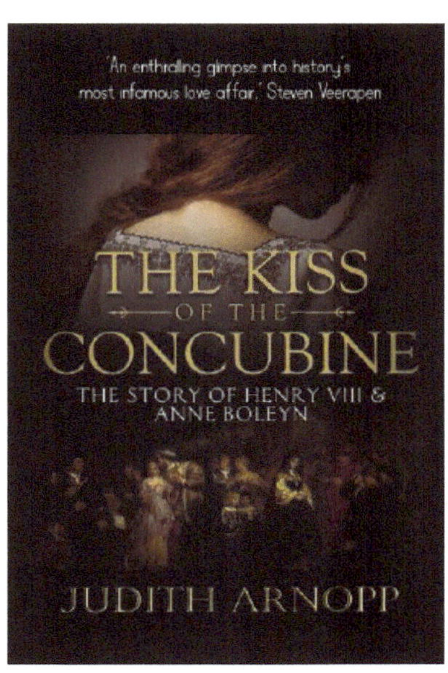

THE KISS OF THE CONCUBINE
by Judith Arnopp

There are moments when, as a reader, you know the second a book impacts you. And when that impact comes at the very beginning, well, you know you are about to take an exquisite journey. I have felt this many times throughout the years and when it happens, the books become dear to me, and a must-have for my own personal library. This is one of those times.

Reading the blurb, one might think this is just another re-telling of the infamous story of Anne Boleyn and Henry VIII, but I am here to say that this book transcends anything I have read to date on this popular subject. When you read lines such as: "...The king's eyes fly open and his eyeballs swivel from side to side, his disintegrating ego peering as if through the slits in a mummer's mask." or "Henry and I are the most powerful couple in all of England and yet, in the face of death, we are powerless," you are compelled to soak in every last detail. And last, I have to share this... "It is a dead sort of day, the type of day where the sky is white, and there is not even the hint of a breeze. Clouds muffle the horizon and I want to push them away, thrust back the oppression and the fear, and revel for one more day beneath blue skies, feel the wind on my cheeks, the scent of Hever in the air. Instead I am here, in my palatial prison, with no future, no next week to look forward to, perhaps not even a tomorrow."

Oh, there are so many many more for you to enjoy on this heavenly journey of words. This is just a small sampling.

The immense beauty of Judith Arnopp's selection of words and phrases is a lesson on how to write a historical novel. She takes what we already know of Anne and Henry to another level, a rare personal glimpse into their personalities, their fears, their hopes, and their love that turned England upside-down in terms of religion. In this book, Anne draws a reader's sympathy, as she is portrayed as a young naïve girl thrust down a path that ultimately brings her ruin. The delicate way the author shows Anne's love for her family home, Hever Castle, and the simplicities of that 'other life', the life before Henry, fleshes out her character and makes her tremendously relatable; as does the bond she shares with her brother, George, that is taken completely out of context by those wishing to destroy her.

The Kiss of the Concubine is now among my 'go-to' books that I will read again and again. Even this review does not do it justice. Simply put... get this book. It is stunning. A must-read!!

*　*　*　*　*

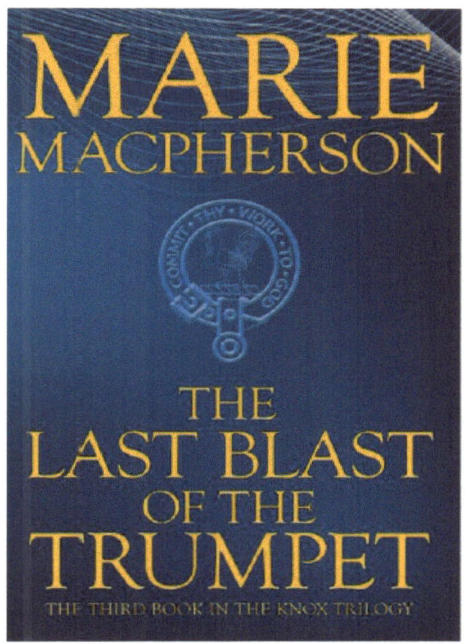

THE LAST BLAST OF THE TRUMPET
by Marie Macpherson

I had to take a few days to really ponder over this review for "The Last Blast of the Trumpet"; to sort of let the words sink in and absorb them into my mind and soul. Another reviewer compared this book to Hilary Mantel's "Wolf Hall" books and to a certain extent I must agree. I adored Mantel's books and while Macpherson's novel, to me, has similarities to her incredible series, there are unique differences that will draw in fans of "Wolf Hall". Such as, the total immersion into the life of John Knox, as Mantel did with Cromwell. I found myself vacillating back and forth between liking his character and not liking his character, the same as I did with the entire novel. There were times I could not put it down and other times I felt tired over the abundance of flourishing words. Abundant but necessary. I admire Macpherson's ability to tackle the atmosphere of the time in the use of the language, having the characters actually speak as they might have spoken by using certain phrasing and verbiage only used by

Editorial Reviews

Scots. For that I say, bravo, Ms Macpherson, for I am a lover of the beauty of words. That being said, I must use a caveat here and say that the tiredness I felt was from an audacious application of alliteration throughout the entire novel. At first I loved it but after the tenth or so time I found myself trying to locate the next alliterative phrase which distracted me from the storyline. However, I'm not sure this will be a hindrance for most, it was just something that irritated me since I am the OCD sort.

Now, for the story itself. As most other reviewers re-summarize the story, I shall just hit the highlights. During the Tudor era, John Knox was the foremost religious reformer and revolutionist against Catholicism, pitting him against Mary, Queen of Scots, and aligning himself with supporters such as Queen Elizabeth of England and her renowned advisor, William Cecil; all against the backdrop of Scotland. I, like most other reviewers, found the sections dealing with his home-life drawing me closer to his character while his religious life made me feel quite the opposite. To this I say, bravo, again, Ms Macpherson for developing such a well-rounded character, a true three-dimensional person who leapt from the page. The other details of the storyline, including the well-known aspects of Queen Mary, were detailed and immersive, revealing things I did not know or bringing them back to mind, such as the fact that Prioress Elisabeth Hepburn was Knox's godmother.

I definitely recommend this read and think anyone who loved Hilary Mantel's books will love this one, as well. It is deep, well-researched, and a good book for reflecting on a powerful and influential man in not only Scottish history but world history. As this is the third in the series and where I began, I am looking forward to going back to book one and two to fill in the rest of the history of his life.

*　*　*　*　*

SONGBIRD
by Karen Heenan

What a way to retell a story about King Henry VIII and Anne Boleyn!! If you've ever wanted to know about the inner workings of the household, told from a servant's POV, one who was closely linked to the infamous King and his wives, well, this is the book to get. This is the story of Bess Davydd, a young girl bought by Henry VIII to become a minstrel for his court, a songstress whose voice is as a nightingales. During the storyline, you are offered brief glimpses and encounters with the royals (i.e. Henry and Anne) but the story is much more about Bess and her love interests – Tom, another bought minstrel, and Nick, a nobleman. The story is compact, well-developed, and stretches into the depths of emotions separating commoners from the high-born, as well as showing the commonality, the human element. If I have one negative, and perhaps it is only from my POV, I struggled with wrapping my head around her age, of how young she is when she starts to experience "love" and with her sounding like a woman at the age of ten to fourteen. I mean, I get it, I know from my own research into history that girls at that age and in that time period were wives and mothers by the time they were fourteen, even younger, but I did struggle a bit with it. However, my own feelings did not overwhelm the overall story, to which I enjoyed thoroughly. I give this book five stars and will highly recommend to anyone who loves books about the Tudor era.

*　*　*　*　*

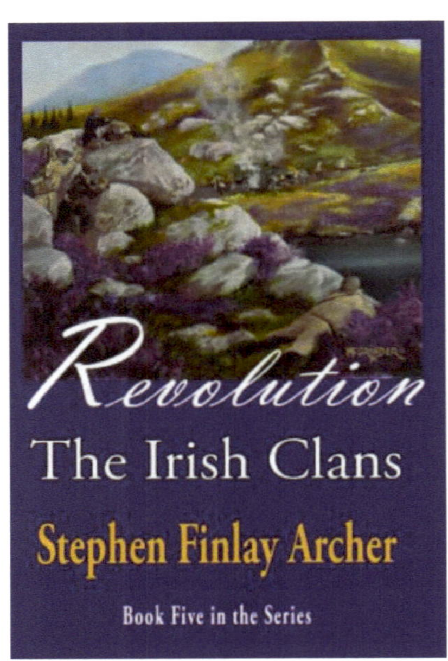

REVOLUTION: THE IRISH CLANS
by Stephen Finlay Archer

He counseled Michael Collins to act as if the Republic was a fact. He would often say, "We defeat the British by ignoring them. As the American John Adams once said, 'Revolution starts in the hearts and the minds of the people.'"

This immersive and jam-packed story begins with the Irish revolution in 1915 and extends to the civil war ending in 1922 to 1923. To say this is epic is putting it mildly, and to just simply note that there are mythological elements which bind the past and the present would not do the book justice.

The author brings to the reader an incredible history of the McCarthy and O'Donnell Clans, and while history tells of their defeat in ancient times, they are by no means extinct. Linked by blood and a medieval pact across the ocean, Ireland and America, the lives of the characters entwine in a quest to support the revolution headed by none other than the infamous Michael Collins. While one part of the family, Collin and Kathy O'Donnell, seek to begin a new life, settling in a home and raising children, in Toronto Canada, another part of the same family, Tadgh and Morgan McCarthy, fight on the front lines to bring freedom to Ireland, fighting alongside Michael and a host of other revolutionaries.

The connection begins with the Black Tom explosion near Ellis Island which damages the Statue of Liberty, a fireball which nearly kills Collin and Kathy... and links Germany to the Irish Clan na Gael who is trying to use the German war to their advantage... that is, to find a way to export guns from America to Ireland for their cause while hiding the shipment under pretense that the guns are going to Britain for the war effort. Enter Tadgh McCarthy.

Tadgh uses his contacts in America while staying with his wife's brother, Collin, to put the deal in motion. All is set and all goes well... at least for a time. Without giving away any spoilers, the author does a remarkable job in revealing the actual history of the time period, the passion and the patriotism fueled in the fiery hearts of Ireland's Gaelic her-

itage... not just during WWI but tracing the roots into the far past where religious myths and divine intervention, where 'luck' plays a role in unearthing a vast Clan treasure, one which funds the revolution.

In one quote from the author, he states that 'readers who are interested in Ireland's struggles for freedom and its storied but often mystical history will enjoy The Irish Clans series. Readers who enjoyed The Da Vinci Code, National Treasure, or Outlander will be enthralled by my stories.' I have to concur his statement, for the essence of all three of those books resonates in just this one book alone, and now I am intrigued to start with book one and read them all.

At the heart of the story is real people who simply want a better life for themselves and their families, and Mr Archer does a remarkable job at offering us well-rounded, passionate characters in extraordinary circumstances. This book is alive with action and lush detail, giving the reader an Irish history lesson wrapped in an intense and captivating story. This is drama to the ultimate level. It has it all – history, adventure, intrigue, war, passion, love, escape, betrayal, sorrow, pain – all the elements which connect us all as humans. This engrossing book is a voice speaking from the past and linking history to the possibilities of myths and the promises of the future.

I began this review with the poignant quote stated to Michael Collins, the quote by John Adams of revolution beginning in the hearts and minds of the people. This vibrant story captures this in every detail – the lengths a person, a country, will go to find freedom from oppression. Every society has its story of freedom. This is Ireland's story, and the implications echo

across generations and across oceans. 'Man's inhumanity to man' screams loud in this book, the sacrifice, the blood, the bravery, and desperation for justice.

From a reader's standpoint, the prose was easy to follow, and very engaging, providing just enough history to infuse knowledge while not diverting from the storyline. Mr Archer is quite the original storyteller, taking elements from all the aforementioned books and crafting a well-told story; however, my one side point is that about halfway through, I felt I was reading two different books. When the storyline veered from Bloody Sunday to the search for the ancient lost medieval treasure, I felt as if I switched books... not so much in engagement and interest (as the story still intrigues) but just in the flow. I understood why the switch was necessary as Archer introduced the mystical Celtic vein, but I did feel like I went from reading "Rob Roy" to "National Treasure." Overall, though, even with the switch, I was always immersed in the story and the development of what happens to the characters and their fight for freedom.

Some of my favorite passages from the book:

The side trip taken by Collin O'Donnell to Independence Hall in Philadelphia when he sees the Liberty Bell - "The impact of liberty, the concept of freedom, resonated. There was damage, that crack, but he took comfort in the fact that history on the side of righteousness had prevailed. Perhaps this would be a model for Ireland."

The brutality and oppression experienced by the revolutionaries - "The IRA had just killed three soldiers in Dublin, the first such deaths in that city

Editorial Reviews

since the battles in the East-er Rising. As a result, Churchill authorized the Black and Tans to begin burning towns and killing civilians. This reminded Griffiths of the slash and burn tactics employed by Cromwell's monsters during the Confederate wars of the sixteen hundreds. Something drastic had to be done."

"God in heaven, this is a tragic day for Ireland." - the presentation of Bloody Sunday is heartbreaking. Michael Collins 'disappears like a ghost into the fog' after Tadgh and Morgan survive the episode at the stadium, and Tadgh vows to him to find a way to continue to help the cause. Thus, he and his wife, Morgan, delve further into their family history in search of the treasure and secrets hidden in the Book of Ballymote.

I am left on the edge of what is to come, and I look forward to continuing the saga with Tadgh and Morgan McCarthy.

Revolution: The Irish Clans, Book Five is awarded five stars by The Historical Fiction Company

*   *   *   *   *

BEHELD: GODIVA'S STORY
by Christopher M. Cevasco

The soughing wind and a wren's whir lulled him, and behind his eyelids he saw her again as she'd revealed herself to him when first he'd come to Coventry late that Eastertide: a lady on a white horse, the morning sun rising behind her as she rode up the High Street. The horse's step had been slow and even, and bathed in that light, she'd seemed clothed in shining, golden silk. Thomas knew at once he'd found his long-sought beacon. A twin half of himself. A worthy haven for his soul.... Some small sound made him start, and Thomas came fully awake, dizzy for a time with the dappled sunlight shifting through the branches. How long have I slept? He looked down. Godgyfu had arrived.

Most everyone knows the ancient legend of Lady Godiva and her naked ride through Coventry, as well as the man who forever was labeled as the "Peeping Tom" in the story, but with Cevasco's novel, the reader is plunged into the depths of a quite deep and murky pond full of scummy characters and dark medieval history as England emerges from the grip of the Danes under King Harthacnut. Godgyfu, Lady Godiva's life is filled with hardship from the very beginning, married at a very young age, which was customary, and emerges from near death to a life under the stringent hand of her husband, who she despises. Yet, her life in service to the community of Coventry, and her monetary and emotional support in building the Abbey, helps keep her focused. She is a deep character, full of flaws and suffocated passions, and ,unfortunately, falls prey to the desires of men in her quest to feel true love.

From the historical aspect, Cevasco does a remarkable job in rendering the true sense of life in this time period, full of gritty blood-soaked battles and a fair share of scoundrels lusting after any woman that moved within their sight. First and foremost, is Godgyfu's husband, Leofric, whose days in battle has turned him into a lecherous old codger whose mind is half filled with voyeuristic imaginings about his own wife, while the other half is filled with mead-induced visions of Saint Paul. This is a world teetering precariously on the edge of devout Christianity while rearing back to the old carnal days of their primitive Celtic roots; a world where women are mere chattel to be done with as the men wish, no matter if they are the local strumpet or the highest noble born woman.

The history of the transition of the kingdom of England from Hathacnut to Eadward is remarkably rich in this story, and unfolds in a similar way to stories such as "Pillars of the Earth" by Ken Follett or books by Bernard Cornwell; not to mention the mingling of religion, politics, and the relationships between men and women which bring to mind "Game of Thrones" by Martin. This book is by no means an easy light read, and the reader should be warned for some graphic battle and sex scenes; however, in delving deeper, the emotional turmoil of this young woman, of Godgyfu, whose inner conflict places her in a very vulnerable position as she falls for a monk novice named Thomas, reveals the author's ability to reach deep into a character's soul and extract an extraordinary narrative. This story is more than blood, guts, and lust... it is about a shattered young girl's desire to be wanted, loved, and accepted. And it reveals the depravity of men who use women for their own ambitions, discarding them at will.

Thomas, the "Peeping Tom", in this story is a piece of work full of machinations in his voyeuristic world with his mind set on recreating Godgyfu as the goddess Rhiannon. He weasels his way into her life and uses her failing marriage as a way to entice her to his bidding, that of carving an image of her in the nude as Marie-incarnate in order to draw the Christians back into their old Pagan ways of worshiping the goddess. He makes a deal with Leofric, Godgyfu's husband, after Leofric discovers the young man watching his wife bathe in the river, and whose own depraved fantasies are ignited upon seeing Thomas watching her. In this story, Thomas is the impetus to Leofric's former impotence, and recharges the Earl's desire for his wife... all at a cost. Both of them use her in order to fulfill their own insatiable greed and desires.

He was such a soft thing beneath all his bluster – wounded somehow – and she wanted to mend him as her husband might have mended one of his falcons with a broken wing. But it was more, she knew. More than only a mothering impulse. She burned for him as she had never before burned for any man.

Then he drew back; he never let things go too far. Only enough to keep pulling her along in her need. And she did need him now, his touch, his words, his nearness..... It was like some men grew to need mead or wine, craving it, living for it. He noticed she'd even begun to shake at times, ever so slightly, another thing he had seen in those for whom drink had become lord and king. Only, for Godgyfu, Thomas himself was her drink, and he doled himself out in forsakingly small draughts.

From a storytelling aspect, this book is first rate. Cevasco has a sensational ability to tell a story rich with beautiful phrasing and well-selected verbiage to give a reader the true sense of character and place. You feel the pain in the hearts or the rain dripping from the beards, you smell the loamy green forests and the pungent urine-drenched streets, you hear the clashing of swords and Godgyfu's cries in the dark, and you can see the love twinkling in her aging eyes as she desperately wants to believe in Thomas's offerings. Cevasco is a remarkable storyteller... enough said. But... I do have to share this last gift of a passage, which, to me, shows the strength of his chosen words in placing a reader firmly into the setting:

A cow lowed outside, a gloomy sound. Cows seemed ever mournful to her, and she tried to call to mind if she'd ever seen a happy one? Wan light leaked past the room's dark beams through a spot of roof thatch wanting mending; daytime them – not night at all. It all felt the same. Poor cows. She suddenly wanted to weep over that frayed bit of thatch.

Beheld: Godiva's Story by Christopher M. Cevasco receives five stars from The Historical Fiction Company and the "Highly Recommended" award for excellence.

* * * * *

THE DOUGLAS BASTARD
by J. R. Tomlin

Under my gambeson, sweat trickled down my sides, and my arms began to ache, but I refused to slow down the steady, careful whack, whack of the wooden blade against the post. Some of the others thought I was unimportant because I was a bastard, but I would prove them wrong. They would see what a bastard could do.

While this outstanding portrayal of intense Scottish history is told from the point-of-view of a young nine-year-old boy thrust quite quickly into manhood, this is by no means young adult fiction; rather, it is a stout homage to other immersive authors like Cornwell who dive into ancient battles with fervour.

Archibald Douglas, the bastard son of Sir James "the Black" Douglas, comes home to Scotland after many years in France serving under King David (also exiled), alongside his father's first cousin, William, 1st Earl of Douglas, Lord Liddesdale, whose intent is to divest Scotland of English souls and send them back to England with their tails tucked

Editorial Reviews

between their legs... or dead. A famous description of Archibald, known as "Black Archibald" is of him being 'dark and ugly more like a cook-boy than a Noble' and yet, he was known as a large man and able to wield a huge sword. As a boy, though, he has something to prove and must overcome the incessant label put upon him and the feeling of unimportance in comparison to his legitimate family members.

We set off, a hundred strong, all wearing long dark cloaks, near nightfall of an October evening with the sun dripping behind wispy gray clouds. A breeze rustled the remaining leaves, crisply curled in brown and gold, that clung stubbornly to the nearly bare branches. Damp litterfall muffled the hoofbeats, and the horses' breath appeared like puffs of smoke. For the first time, Sir William allowed me to carry a sword.

This is a time of knights and jousts, of chivalry and nobility, and a time when Scottish nobles continued to seek independence from English rule since King David's own father, Robert the Bruce, fought alongside William Wallace in this fight. Many of the passages and dialogue betwixt Archie and Will, as well as the scenic passages of Scotland, itself, and the castles hearken back to Randall Wallace's own book Braveheart, not to mention the battle scenes and the constant fear of betrayal by other clans.

Archie begins training as a squire with his eyes set on becoming a knight, of proving his worth not only to Lord Liddesdale but to the King. Again and again, battles rage, blood is spilled, and castles are taken... until he arrives at the Battle of Neville's Cross which spell dire consequences for the King and for Archie's cousin. For a while the reader wonders if Archie and his friend,

Will Ramsay will escape... but Ms Tomlin ties things up in a way to entice the reader onward in anticipation of the next book in this series.

As expected of a hearty full-on historical novel set in 14th century Scotland, the language and brogue is spot-on, and the characters are vivid and fearless while displaying typical human emotion of fear and vulnerability at the appropriate times. You can almost smell the sweat and the peat moss in the descriptions. Ms Tomlin provides outstanding endnotes for the reader to delve a bit deeper into this time period, to distinguish the historical accurate facts woven into the fiction, and to add some new words from the provided glossary into their vocabulary. One caveat in all the richness is the desire for a bit more internal dialogue from Archie – while we get some, and perhaps more later in the next book, the full development of his character felt not quite as deep as needed to connect on all levels, however this by no means dampens the entirety of the storyline, especially for a devout devourer of Middle Age Scottish history. Yet, for the most part, The Douglas Bastard prose is as smooth as a dram of Scotch whiskey and as sharp as a Claymore... an intense read to throw back and slice in one sitting.

I made the sign of the cross and said a quick prayer for Will and me and for the thousands of dead. The English would have been exhausted after the battle, not to mention hours spent looting so many bodies. I ran my hand down my face. I could not think about that. It would unman me.

The Douglas Bastard by J. R. Tomlin receives 5 stars from The Historical Fiction Company

* * * * *

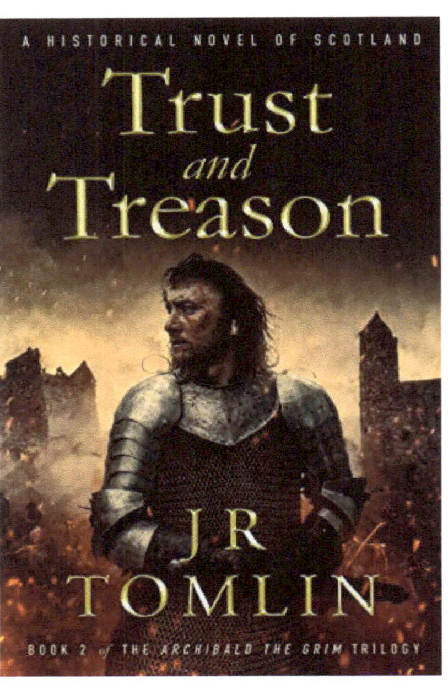

**TRUST AND TREASON
by J. R. Tomlin**

Hugh was my father's last living brother. All his brothers had died in the war, but as the youngest child, he was sent to be a cleric. Some clerics were warlike, but Hugh was not one of them. In the war against England, the Lord of Douglas had a duty to fight. So, at last, he resigned the lordship of Douglas to my cousin, and he had added my name to the entail, making me the heir should all other males in the Douglas line die. Adding a bastard had shocked everyone, including me.

In the continuing story of Archibald Douglas from the previous first book in the series, "The Douglas Bastard", Ms Tomlin engages the reader and builds this enthralling story of a young man, knighted in the first book, trying to discover the correct path of Scotland's future, a tenuous one between trust and treason. After escaping the horrific slaughter at the Battle of Neville's Cross, Archie gathers loyal men and his strength in an attempt to thwart pockets of English soldiers throughout the countryside. His loyalty to the King is fixed, even as he faces questions about his own family's loyalty, and his desire to create a future for himself with a beautiful young lass named Jonetta. Death ravages Scotland as the plague takes hold, sweeping up from London, and Archie continues to build on his chivalric life as a knight, fighting in tournaments and continuing to rout out the pestilent English. His own loyalty is tested when the man he viewed as a father turns traitor... and the result of Archie's decision will set his future course and that of Scotland.

"Robert Stewart and the Earl of Dunbar ran from the battle like dogs with tails between their legs." I leaned over and spit into the rushes on the floor to get the taste of treachery out of my mouth. "They left the rest of us to be slaughtered. Sir William was captured. I dinnae ken how many of his men escaped.... I crawled through the bodies of the slain to escape."

Ms Tomlin again hits the mark in this splendid tale of Scottish history – the historical aspects and the Scottish brogue are woven into the storyline with skill, and the reader is taken even deeper into Archie's mindset and motivations. The descriptive passages of the landscape, of the ravages of the Black Death, and the battles raged paint a clear picture of life in medieval Scotland and the author's skill at world-building is excellent. While the narrative is easily read within one sitting, it is quite immersive with fleshed-out characters which a reader can connect with on a very human and personal level.
All the lords we could have depended on were captured or dead. Sir William pressured my cousin, the Lord of Douglas, to return to Scotland after Hugh resigned the title. I chewed my lip, wondering why Douglas had refused. Most of

this part of Scotland was his land as lord. You would think he would want to be here to claim them.

While "The Douglas Bastard" is as smooth as a dram of Scottish whiskey, "Truth and Treason" is a chaser of rich hearty ale, and is 'highly recommended'.

"It isnae like you are our Lord. If you were the Douglas, that would be different. You'd have the right to call me to your service. But you are nae."
"Aye. I am nae lord." There was no point in mentioning I was a Douglas. I was not the Douglas. "I take your meaning, that your family cannae lose you. Aye, they would turn freeholders into villeins if they could, but driving them out is the only way to stop that. That ends their maltolt as well."

Trust and Treason by JR Tomlin receives 5 stars from The Historical Fiction Company and the 'Highly Recommended" award of excellence.

*　*　*　*　*

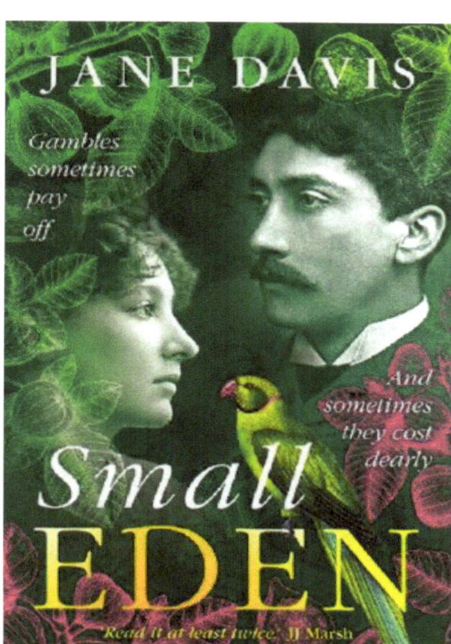

SMALL EDEN
by Jane Davis

By the time the sun sets over the ponds and the herons take to their high nesting places, Robert has established that he has the wherewithal to buy the Reynolds' land – he can create his small Eden.

With all the essence of classic literature, particularly resonating with the voice of Thomas Hardy, this novel emotes the travails and unspoken emotions of the Victorian era. We are first introduced to Robert as a young boy, a boy with dreams of soaring into the clouds in a hot-air balloon, and to his parents, Hettie and Walter, a father who encourages his youthful aspirations and a mother whose past experiences with losing her father at a young age has caused her to lead a very cautious life. When Robert's father tells him the story of a 'ropedancer', a tight-rope walker who nearly plummets to her death over the Thames, the story embeds itself into Robert's life as he grows up, marries Freya (a woman desperate to climb the social classes), and becomes father to two boys and two girls.

In his nocturnal world, his shadow-sons thrive. Thomas is already waist-high, Gerrard not far behind. They age at the same rate as their girls, their Estelle and Ida. He doesn't tell Freya that Thomas has lost a front tooth, or about the faces Gerrard pulls behind his brother's back. Superstition tells Robert he ought to be worried that he sees himself in dreams, but he can't regret this second life he leads, hearing the boys' laughter, watching the delight on their faces. And now he will create for them a place to play.

Yet, this time period is fraught with health dangers, the foremost being scarlet fever... and after "gambling" with his two boys' lives, telling his wife that all is well and no doctor is needed, tragedy strikes this young couple hard. In this world where nothing is talked about and emotions are kept secure under the facade of a stiff upper lip, grief is tamped down and "dealt" with... never discussed. Yet,the pain has a way of niggling its way to the surface, even as the years pass, sometimes in unexpected and harsh ways. Like a small water leak etching its way through rock that eventually breaks boulders.

He grapples with belief as modern men must. Darwin foisted this on them. Outwardly there is no change. His neighbours look as they've always looked, but the seed of doubt has been planted. This life may be all there is. And if that is the case the dead are not waiting, they are just names on lichened headstones to be traced with fingertips. It hollows him out, the thought that he may never meet Thomas and Gerrard again.

Ten years pass, and Robert, a successful businessman in the opium market (medicinal cures of laudanum, etc.), looks for a way to express his silent grief, again without including his wife. While Freya shelters their daughters and pines for inclusion in the social set, Robert buys a piece of land in Carshalton linked to his childhood, a place where he took refuge as a boy, and a place where he imagines his 'shadow-sons' playing. While developing his vision of an Eden-like park, he meets Miss Florence Hoddy, an incredible artist who translates his dream onto paper, securing a hold on his heart with her unabashed openness and having to deal with her own stilted dreams. In dealing with her own pain and tragedy, she teaches the others around her. Florence's way envelopes everyone who meets her – including Robert's mother, Het-

tie (now widowed), Robert's youngest daughter, Ida, who also dreams outside of the box, and the garden caretaker's son, also named Gerrard (of whom Robert begins to treat like a replacement son). In this created world, Robert establishes a newfound family, full of all the emotional support he has needed all along – he buries his grief in the building of this small Eden, all at the exclusion of his wife at times. But not without her own responsibility as she focuses more on the advantages the gardens bring her in society rather than the real reasons behind this creation. Her fault is never taking the opportunity to speak her lost sons' names ever again, or trying to discover the real reason for Robert's obsession with the garden.

The garden envelopes everyone's lives, transforming them in unexpected ways, winding through their lives like ivy, releasing grief's hold while at other times, tightening around throats. Robert walks a tightrope with the financial costs of what his wife considers a folly, and what starts out as a memorial to his sons threatens to crack the foundations of his marriage. Yet, each person involved faces their own change, their own pain, and the author skillfully keeps a grip on the main character, Robert's life, and goals while entwining the lives of the secondary characters. Such as, when Hettie, Robert's mother goes on a quest to Scotland to deal with her own grief of losing her father at an early age, coming back a changed woman, this episode, while away from the happenings in Carshalton, connects Hettie and Robert, linking that same 'itch' that both ultimately feel deep inside, an inheritance passed down from Hettie's parents. Hettie breaks free of the Victorian barrier of showing no emotion, finally telling her son how proud she is of him, as well as other rev-

elations. Freya, on the other hand, fails to let the gardens transform her, even when faced with the widening gulf and possible scandal she embarks upon in the latter part of the novel.

Hettie, always so reluctant, has discovered that she too has restless feet. Perhaps here, words are unnecessary. There's a spiritual aspect to walking that she hadn't anticipated. The rocks themselves are possessed of spirit. For the first time in as long as she can remember Hettie is at peace, with herself and her surroundings. Here one can observe the daily rotations of the heavens. It is possible, even, to believe in God.

The author's love for this cottage, Rossdale Cottage, the former ticket office and entrance to Clarke's Pleasure Gardens, is quite evident, and is a tribute to the many places people find themselves attached to which hold within the roots an incredible historical story. The world around such places build up, modernizes, develops, and much history is lost, but remarkable authors such as Ms Davis, with her brilliant writing and painstaking research, bring not only the characters to life but the places, as well. The passages are breathtaking with deep meaning and structure, the characters are alive and breathing, full of self-doubt, honesty, pain, love, and struggle – all very human qualities of which any reader can connect with. Her tender care of what it means to lose a child, or children, and how avoiding grief can cause cracks in any relationship is quite noteworthy... as well as the need to memorialize the loss in a profound way speaks to this reviewer's heart. As a mother who lost two, as well, before undertaking grief counseling, for a time it was my fervent desire to create a garden to memorialize my 'shadow-children', and both my husband and I have grieved in our own individual ways while maintaining our emotional connection. Grief can wreck lives, as the author so clearly depicts, and makes you question so much, but finding your balance, of releasing the grip and finding a soft place to land, does much to heal. Bravo, Ms Davis, bravo for the life lessons and history embedded in this sensational book!

It was here, in the cottage, that I would first entertain the thought that I might one day write a novel, and I would live for that notion for a long time, turning it over and over, before I finally dared to say the words out loud. Because it has been a rule of mine since childhood: once you say something out loud, a bargain is struck.

Small Eden by Jane Davis receives five stars and the "Highly Recommended" award of excellence from The Historical Fiction Company.

*   *   *   *   *

INFANTS OF THE BRUSH: A CHIMNEY SWEEPS STORY by A. M. Watson

Infants of the Brush by A. M. Watson is an honest-to-goodness atmospheric depiction of life on the London streets for the young chimney sweep boys during the 1700s, and just as the blurb describes, the stories resonates tones of Dicken's story of "Oliver Twist". This homage is true to form in the style of the narrative, usage of dialect, and setting, as well as the development of the characters and world-building. Comparison to Dickens, while not to some people's taste as Dickens is an acquired taste for many, the similarities puts this story right up there with his classic tales of poverty and strife on the mean streets of Georgian London.

We are introduced to the life of a sweep through Egan, sold at six-year-old by his destitute mother to a Master Broomer, Daniel Armory, who uses the boys in his care to clean the chimneys of the city while lining his pockets with coin. Often referred to as "apprentices", they were actually "indentured slaves" without a means to escape the life unless purchased out with five guineas or by reaching an age and height too big to climb the flues. Egan finds himself 'chained' to this life after his father dies at sea and his sister is suffering from a life-threatening fever which forces his mother to give him away since she cannot afford to take care of him any longer. Yet, you get a sense of Egan's hopefulness when he first peers out across the rooftops of London.

"Now sweep the chimney out, you sot!" Pitt yelled and disappeared into the chimney stack.

"I did it!" Egan whispered to himself as he surveyed his field of victory. London's rooftops spread out before him, bathed in the full light of morning. Egan dangled at the top of the world among the birds that glided upon the wind. Specks of people trod upon the streets below. They could not reach him. They could not look down on him. For a moment, he exceeded their station.

In the gang of sweepers, he meets Pitt, who takes him under his wing, teaches him the ropes of climbing, of cleaning, along with his own learned life lessons along the way. The author is quite skilled in describing and immersing the reader into the scenes, oftentimes you can truly get a sense of the smells and thickness of the soot on their grimy little faces.

The poem by William Blake "The Chimney Sweepers" truly comes to life in this story:

"When my mother died I was very young,
And my father sold me while yet my tongue,
Could scarcely cry weep weep weep weep.
So your chimneys I sweep and in soot I sleep"

"That's yer problem, Pitt. You can't see beyond the walls of this cellar, but we're almost out of here whether we have five guineas or not. Master Armory don't keep broomers much past fourteen, and I'm almost too big for flues anyway. We need a plan. What if he sells us to the Americas?" Will argued. "I have me own plans." "Well, I knew life before sweeping and sure as spit I'll see life afterward."

The court case which develops in this story line, that of 'Armory vs Delamirie' (a real case) is melded into the storyline flawlessly, and is a court case which brings to light the issues of child labor. The facts of the case, which lay the foundation of this story, are that a chimney sweeper's boy, Egan, finds a jewel and carries it to the defendant, Paul de Lamerie, an actual renowned silversmith in the 18th century, to find out what the jewel was and upon delivery, the apprentice of Lamerie, the fictional Charles Greville, removes the stones and insists on paying the sweep a mere pittance of what it was actually worth. Egan refuses and asks for the jewel back, thus resulting in the court case between his master, Daniel Armory, and the shop owner, Paul de Lamiere, as well as the further implications of the 'finders keepers' law which is still being used today.

The remarks of "precious child" and "such a dearie" fell flat on his ears. Women like these never noticed broomers on the streets. They only cared for him because of his clean skin and fine clothes. No one helped him when Pitt died. No one cared for Pitt or called him a "dear child." Egan could not hide his disgust when Missus Armory pinched his cheeks and called him her "sweet fire imp."

Court case aside, the overall theme of the book, that of friendship, hope, and survival resonates throughout the narrative, and shines a light on the horrible conditions children suffered during that time... and brings to the forefront that many such ones still suffer in our modern world. History does indeed repeat itself when no one learns from the past. Egan, from the time he climbs the very first chimney to the time he peers across the wide expanse of ocean on a sailing ship, looks to the hopeful horizon, and his inspiring story soaks deep into the reader's heart. You cannot help but feel incredible empathy for the characters, as well as amazement at the author's literary skill in this not-to-be-missed debut novel.

Egan lifted his eyes. Surrounded by a vast expanse of water, the ship rocked along the endless line of waves that crested and crashed into the sea below. Egan was a wee seed pearl compared to the ocean that stretched out before him, but he was a part of it. He was a part of it, and his heart could hear its call. It was just as his Da had said. Egan was at home among the water.

Infants of the Brush by A. M. Watson receives five stars from The Historical Fiction Company and the "Highly Recommended" award of excellence.

* * * * *

A LIGHT AMONG US: CORNWALL
by Jill George

"It is a good things that you and your family do to aid the less fortunate. You have the spirit of God flowing though you. It is as if a light of goodness shines through you. Through your donations, it is as if you are helping us see there is a light among us."

For fans of the Poldark series, and lovers of all things involving Cornwall, this beautiful book relays the story of Elizabeth Carne, a fascinating and remarkable 19th-century woman who was ahead of her time and laid the foundation for incredible educational and geological programs during that time period, based in her hometown of Penzance.

In the opening, at fifteen-years-old, she is already a fountain of knowledge, supporting her father, a well-known banker and geologist, spouting forth her opinions and answering questions with very forthright answers on an excursion to St Michael's Mount. This preview of Elizabeth's intellect sets the stage for the entirety of the book, revealing a very strong-minded young woman whose legacy, as her father instills in her, to become the first woman banker of Cornwall, and a forceful voice in the world of geology. Although she is a heiress, she uses her good fortune as a means for philanthropic pursuits, for the betterment of the people of Cornwall, especially the miners, the farmers, and the children who lack in any sort of education. Yet, this pursuit leaves her quite alone, unable to settle into a normal relationship with a man, in particular Henry Pearce, a man below her station but who connects with her on a very deep level.

"The differences in classes create isolation and monotony of thought and feeling, and then prejudice and class differences separate us from justice." I will look to how much I have learned from Henry, the Freethy family – and yes, even Mr Richards – and also the perceptions of my friend Betsy the baker, the miners and the ball maidens, to enrich my book here and I am all the better for knowing these people and their abilities and perspectives. I see how others in the world could also benefit.

As Elizabeth grows up, and matures, taking on more and more responsibility in the bank, in writing weighty articles about the problems of social inequality and the lack of education, as well as her geological findings, her hasty rejection of Henry has him pursuing and marrying another young lady in the town, a woman who involves herself with some unsavory characters involved in smuggling, a blight upon the Penzance community. Elizabeth, herself, has several run-ins with the main smuggler, yet she is able to maintain her calm and continue shining as a moral and upright citizen whose Methodist upbringing and her own solid visions help her to overcome quite a few tragedies throughout her life. She is determined to uphold her promise to her father to ensure the family's legacy even in the midst of economic hardships (the downturn of the mining industry), unbearable poverty surrounding her, the restrictive society tightened like a corset around women, and the sudden freedom given to her after the men in her life (her father, grandfather, and brothers) depart in one way or another.

I will blend these together as examples for my book. I will entitle it, Country Towns and the Place they fill In Modern Civilization." I will solicit reactions from Bell and Daldy, publishers in London, and ask them to publish it, if they are favorable. I believe these were the publishers my cousins, the Brontës, used, but I will confirm.

The historical research woven into this tale is astounding, and the educational aspect about this woman whose story might have been lost to time if not for Ms George's dedication for revealing the importance of her life, is quite noteworthy in light of the fact that Elizabeth's cousins, the Brontë sisters in Yorkshire are quite well-known in relation to her story. Ms George is to be commended for bringing Elizabeth's life to the forefront in such a superb narrative. Ms George even gives us an exciting twist in the relationship between Elizabeth and Henry, a fictitious relationship, but one that works well into the storyline involving smuggling rings, lies, and murder, and represents, as the author notes, the true love the people of Cornwall had with the incredible woman. This book is highly recommended.

Nothing in this world made me happier than these cliffs that looked as if a giant had taken an enormous spade or axe and hewn them along the coast like cutting a piece of cake. I wanted to burn this fresh happy day in my memory to recall during times of sadness in the future. I was hesitant to truly feel happiness when it did come along because it seemed profound sadness was always just around the corner. I tried to keep a happy, positive outlook and insisted to myself that a day like today was one of life's jewels.

The Light Among Us: Cornwall by Jill George receives five stars and the "Highly Recommended" award of excellence.

*　*　*　*　*

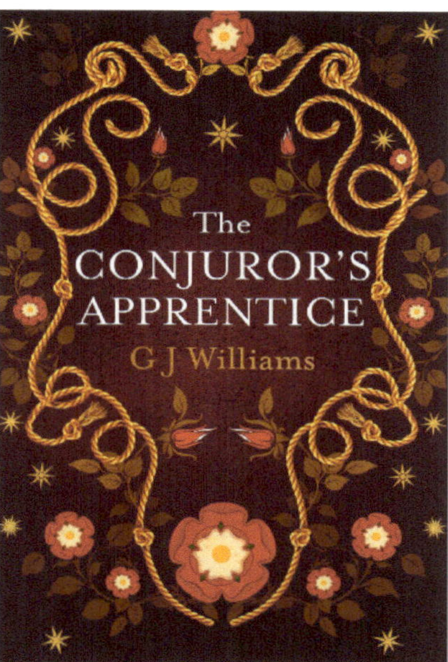

THE CONJURER'S APPRENTICE
by G. J. Williams

One day, the body of a stable boy serving Lord Cecil's household shows up on the banks of the river Thames in London with a yellow woolen ribbon on his body. John Dee, a mathematician and astronomer is called to investigate the corpse and explore the circumstances. By his side is Margaretta Morgan, a young apprentice disguised as a maid.

It is 1555 London, and the rumor is that Mary Tudor, the queen of England, is pregnant and expected to give birth soon. Her sister Elizabeth has been summoned to assist and witness the birth, thus giving up any hopes that one day she may claim the throne for herself. Queen Mary, who had restored Catholicism in the English kingdom, had married prince Philip of Spain, whom she loved very much.

These are the settings of G.J. Williams's murder mystery novel, The Conjuror's Apprentice, where the detective is a sorcerer and his apprentice an empath, abilities both dangerous and thrilling.

From the first pages, I knew the book was different from other crime books I read, not only because it takes place in 16th century England, a time of turbulence and struggles for power, but because Margaretta, the protagonist, has a rare talent. This she needs to cultivate on the street of London, witnessing the persecution and execution of believers of the Protestant faith that opposed the Catholics. When he sends her out, her teacher John Dee thinks this is the best way to learn.

"If you are to hone your gift, you have to understand the full spectrum of men's feelings, fears, and fallacious thoughts.

Great Britain, Scotland, Ireland Edition

The good, the evil, the kind, the cruel, the intelligent and the witless. It is all part of our soul and you need to see them all."

Thus, she can help John Dee solve the mystery and expose the criminal. But the crimes continue as the two uncover clues incriminating royal family members and overseas spy agents. Their investigation relies only on interviewing witnesses and collecting evidence. None of the modern forensic techniques were available to them. But what they have proved to be more valuable: a handful of crystals and a deck of tarot cards, mastered by John Dee, and the gift of mind reading that Margaretta possesses. They use these tools only sparsely as they can also kill.

With a keen eye for historical accuracy, the author portrays her characters with a fine brush, giving them distinct personalities and strong voices. Our protagonist, Margaretta, is only nineteen years old, but she's witty and humble at the same time. And when the stakes are high, by the end of the book, her courage saves not only the day but the future of the English royalty. But Margaretta is not an ordinary girl, and she knows it.

"The doctor did my cards the day he found me and they told him I am an old soul. In the religion of our ancestors, they would believe I have been born many times and had walked this earth before in numerous guises. But we dare not to speak of such things these days for fear of being called heretic, conjuror, witch...all the names which strike fear into the soul in Queen Mary's terrible reign."

And indeed, these esoteric methods help Doctor Dee and Margaretta investigate and solve the series of crimes, and the two of them struggle to keep it a secret as their lives and loved ones' lives depend on it. But such gifts must come out and shine sooner or later, and that is when the plot diverges, higher stakes being now at play. However, the author skillfully ties up loose ends and stirs the readers to an ending that, although predictable to a history buff, has a satisfying ending and promises that the characters may return in another book in the series.

The novel is written in an alert and assertive tone, with episodes of inner dialog, and it is clear of unnecessary descriptions or filler dialog that sometimes clutter a book. To portray the people in their historical context, the author often uses historical details rather than archaic words, sometimes with an amusing result like this:

"Just as before, Lottie refused to wash as it was a church day. Not even Margaretta's insistence that she should try to smell sweet for Sam would shake her fear of water on Sundays."

G. J. Williams mastered the arching plot and character development by layering the subplots and intertwining the secondary characters, improving the storyline and making the experience more gratifying. And because the book is a well-crafted mystery with elements of romance, set in a thoroughly researched historical period, with some real characters, I would recommend the book to any reader of historical fiction.

The Conjurer's Apprentice by G. J. Williams receives five stars and the "Highly Recommended" award of excellence from The Historical Fiction Company

Use the QR code to have your historical novel editorially reviewed and/or enter the HFC Book of the Year Contest

THE HISTORICAL FICTION COMPANY

www.thehistoricalfictioncompany.com

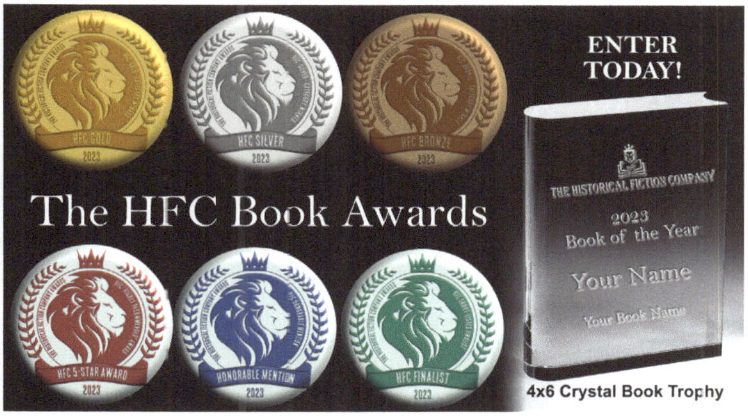

ENTER TO WIN
$1000 CASH PRIZE
plus Book Marketing

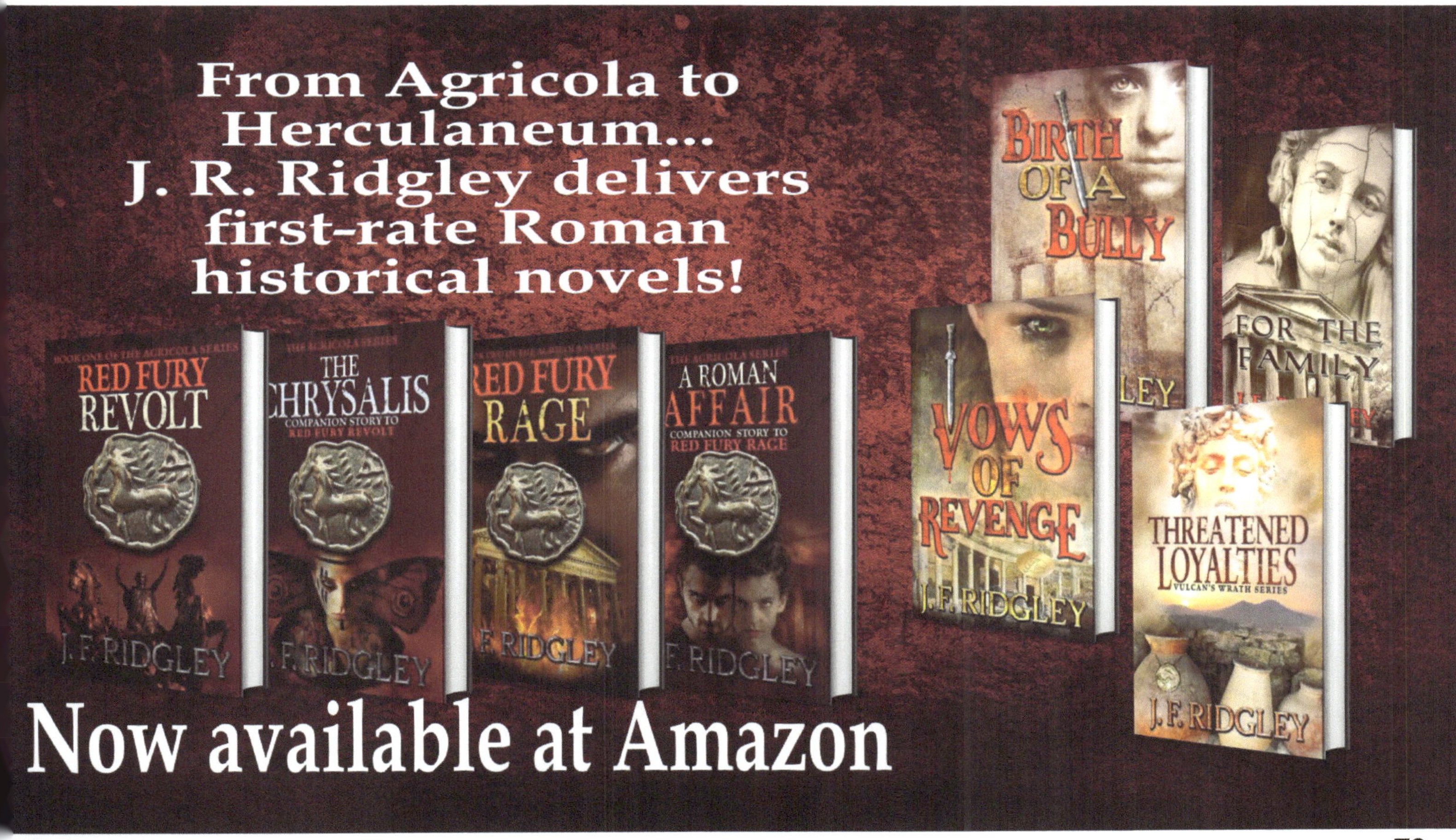

Check out the newest episodes from the History Bards podcast, available for audio listening at Spreaker, Spotify, and iHeartRadio - just search "History Bards" and don't forget to subscribe to hear all our episodes which will post weekly on Tuesdays at 8:00 am EST.

We have an exciting first season which will run until December 2023, featuring historical authors from around the world, and history-filled content episodes based on author's historical novels.

DANIEL GREENE's Author Interview

Author of the Northern Wolf Series

Youtube:

MORAL FIBRE CONTENT EPISODE

Featuring Helena P. Schrader's WWII Novel

Youtube:

ALINA RUBIN's Author Interview

Author of the Hearts and Sails Series

Youtube:

SARAH V. BARNES' Author Interview

Author of "She Who Rides Horses"

Youtube:

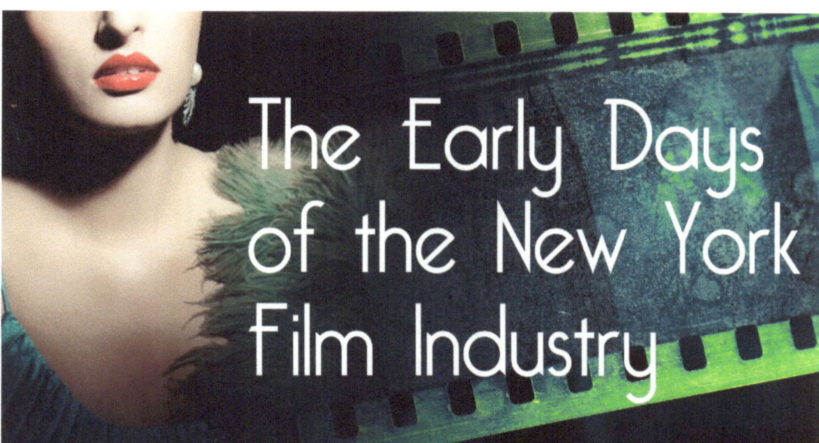

SUSANNE DUNLAP's Author Interview

Author of "The Courtesan's Daughter"

RELEASING April 25th, along with a fascinating content episode on the 27th featuring Susanne's book!

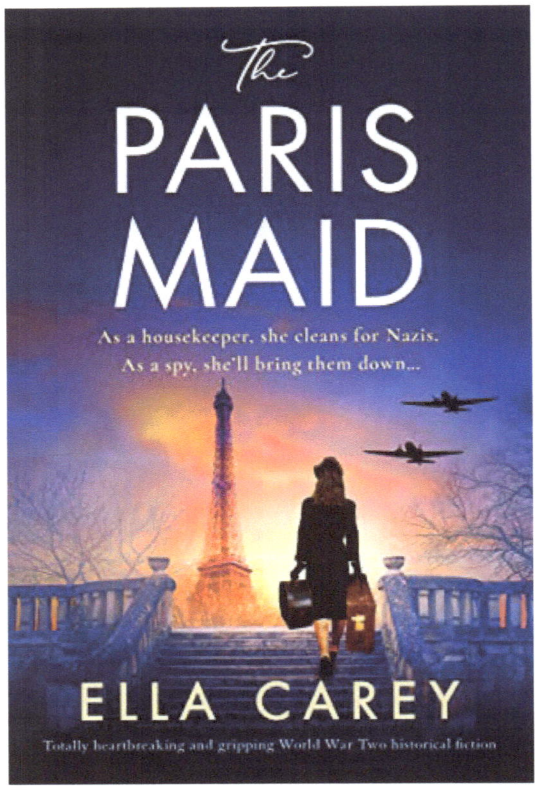

THE TRANSFORMATIVE POWER OF HISTORICAL FICTION

Totally heartbreaking and gripping World War Two historical fiction!

"The Paris Maid" by Ella Carey Now at AMAZON

www.ellacarey.com

While historical fiction has the ability to transport us to another time and another place, for me, one of the most powerful aspects of writing and researching my most recent novel The Paris Maid, is the fact that it has transformed the way I feel about Paris for good.

Now, when I look at photographs of the areas in the city where I set the novel, I find myself incredibly moved in ways that I have not properly understood or felt before. Writing and researching this book has brought my respect and compassion for the people who lived in Paris between 1940 and 1944 to an entirely different level again. It has given me a far greater depth of understanding of what Paris suffered, and an appreciation for the beauty, grace and courage that epitomises the city, and was never allowed to die.

I am certain that next time I go to Paris, and sit outside at one of the sidewalk cafés, I will not just be thinking about food, and art and people watching. No. I will be imagining what it was like for my characters to walk the streets of the city with not only incredible courage, under the watchful eyes of the Nazis, but with constant fear laced in their hearts.

However, it was setting my novel in the iconic Ritz hotel in Paris' luxurious place Vendome, that has really deepened my understanding of the complexities that were brewing in Paris toward the end of the Second World War.

The Ritz was officially a neutral hotel, because it was owned by Swiss proprietors, and therefore was not supposed to be on one side or the other. However, this did not deter the Nazis from taking full advantage of one of the most beautiful and opulent buildings in occupied France.

From the Imperial suite, decorated with silk canopies, and exquisite furnishings, Goering orchestrated the blitz, along with some of the most reprehensible acts that occurred during the Second World War. Coco Chanel lived in the other side of the hotel with her German lover, the Nazi, Hans Günther von Dincklage. But one of the most fascinating characters I found while carrying out my research was the film star, Arletty, who throughout her lengthy career as an actress, had moved from dance halls, to theatres, to pictures, culminating in her playing some of the silver screen's most iconic roles. Arletty also tucked herself away in the Ritz for the duration of the war, forming a liaison with Luftwaffe officer, Hans-Jürgen Soehring. Ultimately, it was Arletty who fascinated me, and so she became a character in my book.

But as soon as the Nazis moved into the Ritz, the French guests were moved from the grander place Vendome side of the hotel to the slightly less exuberant rooms that looked over the Rue Cambon. Top ranking Nazis moved into the suites overlooking the place Vendome, and filled the restaurants and bars with what was often regarded as indiscreet chatter, overheard by many of the Ritz's loyal staff. The hotel was like a cauldron on the boil. In a situation that was officially neutral, everybody had to choose a side. Many people were double crosses, and it is said that the place Vendome was filled with spies.

In the bar on the rue Cambon side of the hotel, legendary barman Frank Meier oversaw a string of resistance activities. The manager of the hotel, Claude Auzello orchestrated the widespread underground network amongst the staff in the hotel. His wife, Blanche, was an important figure in the French resistance, only to be captured by the Nazis in the summer of 1944. Blanche felt wonderful. She had to go into my novel as well.

However, ultimately I wanted to explore what it might have been like not to be one of the grand and illustrious guests in the hotel. I wanted to write from the perspective of someone decidedly un-grand in a grand setting. Someone who, if I had not written about them, might slip behind the scenes. Louise Bassett, therefore is a maid working in the Ritz hotel. She has an excellent memory for numbers and attracts the attention of Frank Meier, who asks her to join the underground network that is operating amongst the staff.

Frank is initially interested in the fact that Louise can remember strings of numbers, words and statistics without any effort at all. She can recall which Nazis stayed in which rooms on which dates, and who visited them. The underground network in the Ritz hotel operated by sending coded messages to the Allies in neutral territories informing them which Nazis were staying in the hotel and when.

For Louise, the opportunity to do something truly brave while using her extraordinary memory is an offer that is too tempting to turn down. What's more, she wants to be recognised for more than her abilities with numbers and letters. Here is her chance to truly be part of something human and real.

While Louise may only be a simple maid, she has eyes and ears everywhere. She is the perfect person to be a spy, because she knows how to scuttle around the hotel without drawing any attention to herself. Who is more invisible than a maid? While Arletty has become famous by drawing attention to herself,

Louise has done the opposite.

At times, the Nazis were known by vegetable codenames. Louise thinks it is hilarious that Goering is referred to as a potato! In her daily rounds, she cleans his magnificent Imperial suite, running her fingers through his bowls filled with sapphires and rubies and emeralds, and dusting around his saucers filled with illicit amphetamines.

Arletty comes to trust Louise, and this becomes problematic. Louise is drawn into Arletty's complicated relationship. But when a Jewish friend of the once famous actress is murdered at the hands of the Nazis, Arletty is forced to make a choice that ultimately is going to determine her own fate. For the lives of the women in the Ritz, life was never going to be the same again once the Allies arrived. Seeing all of this drama through the eyes of a maid was fascinating, but then, my maid Louise was faced with an impossible dilemma of her own. Her life took a strange turn, and suddenly, she was thrust into the spotlight of her own story, even though she had tried to hide away in the hotel from her past.

But it was outside the Ritz that the true tragedy of the war was playing out in the homes of Paris. Starving, freezing through long winters, and not able to afford to buy clothes or shoes for their families, the terror that the citizens of Paris must have felt in their everyday lives seems to be all but wiped clean from the Paris we know now. It's certainly not something I ever thought about when I first visited Paris as a teenager, or even on subsequent visits, not having looked so emotionally at what happened there during World War II.

And I think this is the power of historical fiction. It is an emotional art form that is unique because it is about being able to inhabit a person from the past and understand their hearts and minds, and the decisions they had to make.

In the Paris Maid, my story threads outside the city as well into the northern countryside of France, where an Allied air force pilot must abandon his plane. He parachutes straight into St Germain-en-Laye, and is thrust into the countryside of France, forced to rely on the kindness of the underground network, in order, simply to survive.

This part of the novel for me, is again, an intensely personal story. My father was an Allied air force pilot during the Second World War. He dropped parachutists over France to aid in the French resistance, and reading accounts of what they saw, experienced, and felt was also an incredibly moving experience for me.

Again, it is that sense of place that I find so overwhelming and powerful in writing historical fiction. Imagine hearing the sound of a prop engine on an aircraft groaning and grinding like a sinking ship as it is about to go down, the way the whole plane would have shuddered, and the shaky view of the patchwork fields of France spreading out below as you opened your silver parachute and headed straight into Nazi ground.

Paris, for me is now enhanced. More beautiful, more fascinating, more layered and moving and complex. For I truly think that it is only through historical fiction that we can really begin to feel the past. This is one of the true inspirations for me, and one of the most powerful reasons why I write.

AN INTRODUCTION TO THE WAR OF THE ROSES

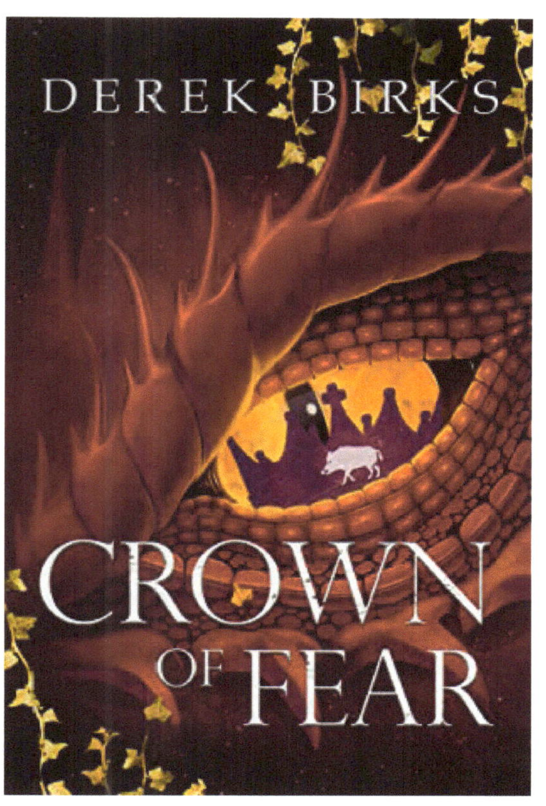

On a marshy plain not far from Market Bosworth the fate of the Elders and the kingdom of England will finally be settled.

"Crown of Fear"
(Book 9 - War of the Roses Series)
Now at AMAZON

When I talk to people about the Wars of the Roses, their eyes often glaze over as they prepare for the inevitable flood of dates and events about people who only ever seem to be called Edward, Henry or Richard. In other words, they expect to be confused; so, I have spent several years attempting to bring some clarity to a period that is often seen as labyrinthine in its complexity.

But, if you don't start with dates and events, where do you start? Well, my historical rule of thumb tells me that if you want to understand an event of this scope it's always as well to look at what came before. So let's explore what happened to England in the century before the fifteenth when the Wars of the Roses took place.

England in the second half of the fourteenth century was a society in flux: a people battered and bruised, a country struggling to come to terms with what had been hurled at it in the middle of the century: the Black Death. The Black Death was the greatest plague Europe had ever seen and it tore a gaping wound in the body of the English nation. The Death struck at rich and poor alike, the low born and the high born. People died on an unimaginable scale — how could men and women ever make sense of their lives again after that? This disaster asked searching questions not only of people's faith, but also of their place in the very fabric of society.

After the Death, widespread famine followed, the economy was sent reeling and the ruling classes panicked: passing strict laws in a futile attempt to bolster up the creaking feudal system. As if this wasn't enough, the ongoing Hundred Years War against France drained England's resources. War was expensive, so harsh taxes were levied to pay for it and in 1381 the peasants rose up in their thousands in an unprecedented revolt against the hated Poll Tax — a tax on everyone in England. This Peasants' Revolt threatened to shake the crown from the very head of young Richard II. He survived it but by the turn of the century

England was still in turmoil: there was faction, usurpation and rebellion and when the dust settled on the bloody battlefield of Shrewsbury in 1403, the House of Lancaster was left in control of England in the person of King Henry IV.

What would happen next? The nation held its breath…but at first it seemed that normal service had been restored when Henry IV passed on the throne to his son, the young warrior king, Henry V of Agincourt fame. He achieved the seemingly impossible by reviving English fortunes in the war with France, cutting a swathe through French lands and finally imposing a treaty by which he expected, sooner or later to become king of France. English pride had been given a mighty boost.

And at home on the lower rungs of the social ladder, life was beginning to present a few opportunities that had rarely been possible before the Black Death. Now, a simple labourer might work for wages and, if he earned enough, he might become a tenant farmer and then who knows, he might sell produce for a small profit. He still did not have any political voice, but he might just be able to improve his lot in life.

On the national stage, however, the optimism was short-lived for, when Henry V died young in 1422, he left a male heir barely 9 months old. For the next 65 years, England was dominated by a succession of powerful nobles and the factions they gathered about them. During that period the problems of government mounted: the French war started to go badly and at home the rule of law gradually broke down. By the 1450s the fragile king, Henry VI and his disgruntled nobles were obliged to settle their differences on the battlefield.

When I was a student of history, I recall that the fifteenth century used to be referred to as the 'decline of the Middle Ages' as if society stood still or stagnated and as if progress was somehow stalled whilst the land was ravaged by conflict until rescued by the arrival of the Renaissance. This of course was a load of tosh because, though the fifteenth century had its share of chaos, it was also a time of opportunity. England was not in decline: many towns grew, trade flourished and thus the business of government became more complex – too complex by far for a king to control it any longer by the sheer force of his personality – especially if, like Henry VI, he didn't have very much personality to start with.

So now let's take a brief look at the leading players in what became the original 'game of thrones.'

My first taste of these personalities was, I suspect like quite a few other folk, through the history plays of William Shakespeare. But although the plays introduced me to some of what we might call the "Hollywood stars" of the period, they remained pretty shadowy figures until I began to undertake a bit of research for myself. What I learned in the course of that research is that studying the politics of fifteenth century England is not for the faint-hearted. There was an absolute feast of riveting personalities, savage battles, sudden switches of allegiance, violent feuds, the murder of innocents – and not so innocents - and Lord knows what other mayhem. You could find yourself up to your elbows in blood and gore…

Strangely, at the centre of all this catastrophic carnage was a vacuum: a weak king. Henry VI was a man with all the charisma of a sponge and the good sense of a lemming. Around him clustered the main players of the political game, the purveyors of power and intrigue. These were the leading members of the great noble houses of England: York, Lancaster, Beaufort, Neville, Percy and so on. These prominent men and women existed against a colourful tapestry of ambition, betrayal and violence – such twists and turns, you couldn't read about it! Except of course you could, because the dodgy characters and double-crosses are perfect territory for historical novelists like me.

The name the Wars of the Roses – coined several centuries after the events – suggests a period of constant war but, as some historians have been at pains to point out, the fighting was far from continuous. However, whilst it was sporadic it was also pretty explosive and some of the early battles had far-reaching consequences. In the first Battle of St Albans in 1455, for example, the deaths of several key noblemen created personal feuds that would fester on for at least another generation as sons vowed to avenge their fathers. Battles sometimes killed off the leaders of one generation of combatants, only to clear the way for their sons to ratchet up the competition a notch or two - what drama!

The battles themselves have also attracted a lot of interest because they were frequently quite bloody. The way men fought had evolved by the mid-fifteenth century into a blood and guts contest: two opposing ranks of well-armoured men at arms wielding heavy swords, axes and maces on foot. They would hack away at each other until physical – or metal – fatigue decided the outcome. Archers were still a lethal ingredient and to add an extra bit of spice there were handguns and cannon. These new weapons could be dangerous both to the victim and the user but they were there to stay and could not be ignored. It was not simply the means of warfare which led to so many casualties; it was also the mind-set of the participants and their battlefield commanders. In an effort to finish their epic struggle once and for all, the cry of 'no quarter' was heard on a number of fields, notably at the bloodiest battle of Towton in 1461.

Bringing even more chaos to the battlefield was the glorious English weather which managed to extract a few startled rabbits from hats. For example, before Mortimer's Cross - fought on a cold February morning in 1461 - there was a remarkable parhelion – a vision of three suns formed by a combination of the dawn light and ice crystals in the air - that doesn't happen every day! The decisive battle of Towton began in a snow blizzard and at Barnet they were fighting in a fog so dense they could not tell friend from foe. Since the latter two battles were pivotal to the outcome of the Wars of the Roses, it is interesting that in both the weather played a significant role.

In recent years much more has been written about some of the period's more prominent women – not only in historical fiction, but also in the work of historians themselves. We now know a little more about these women and the part they played in the politics of the period and the more we know, the more we realise how much we don't know.

Possibly the most dramatic phase of the 'Wars' kicked off after the untimely death of Edward IV in 1483, leaving two young male heirs. This provoked a power struggle between the dead king's brother, Richard, Duke of Gloucester and the family of the queen, the Woodvilles. In that struggle, Richard has forever been cast as the villain, but for generations the charge has been disputed. Did he kill his nephews? Did he kill his wife? Did he kill his brother, Clarence? Did he kill anyone at all? Is there anyone he didn't kill?

Or perhaps he was just an earnest plodder who was a bit unlucky. Either way, it has always seemed to me that if he was a villain then then he was not very good at it. You would think that after over 500 years the world would have had its fill of Richard III but no - excavate a car park and up he popped – and the controversy was reignited.

People are immediately drawn to the man and the public interest seems unlikely to wane any time soon. Such fascination with interesting people and what they did in difficult circumstances is timeless. Indeed, the Wars of the Roses, as a whole, seems such a great soap opera. At each stage in the drama, just when it appeared that peace had been secured, another crisis came along and all the old rivalries, as well as a few new ones rose to the surface.

By the time Henry Tudor became king at the end of it all, most of his potential rivals had gone. But even then he was still not safe because, although all the real male heirs appeared to be dead, a few imposters turned up – or were they imposters?

The Wars of the Roses is one of the great stories of English History so, if you are interested in finding out more you might like to check out my series of 46 short podcast episodes which seek to explain the whole sorry conflict. These are free and available from my website – www.derekbirks.com/podcast/ or any podcast provider.

Derek Birks
www.derekbirks.com

Derek is interested in a wide range of historical themes but began his writing career with the late medieval period. He writes action-packed fiction which is rooted in accurate history. His debut historical novel, Feud, is the first of a series of books entitled The Wars of the Roses which follows the fortunes of the fictional Elder family.

You can follow him on Twitter as @Feud_writer and his author page on Facebook is: www.facebook.com/feudwriter. To find out more about his books, or to contact him you can go to his website: www.derekbirks.com and he also has an occasional blog: www.dodgingarrows.wordpress.com.

FOR MORE HISTORICAL BLOG POSTS,
visit www.thehistoricalfictioncompany.com/blog

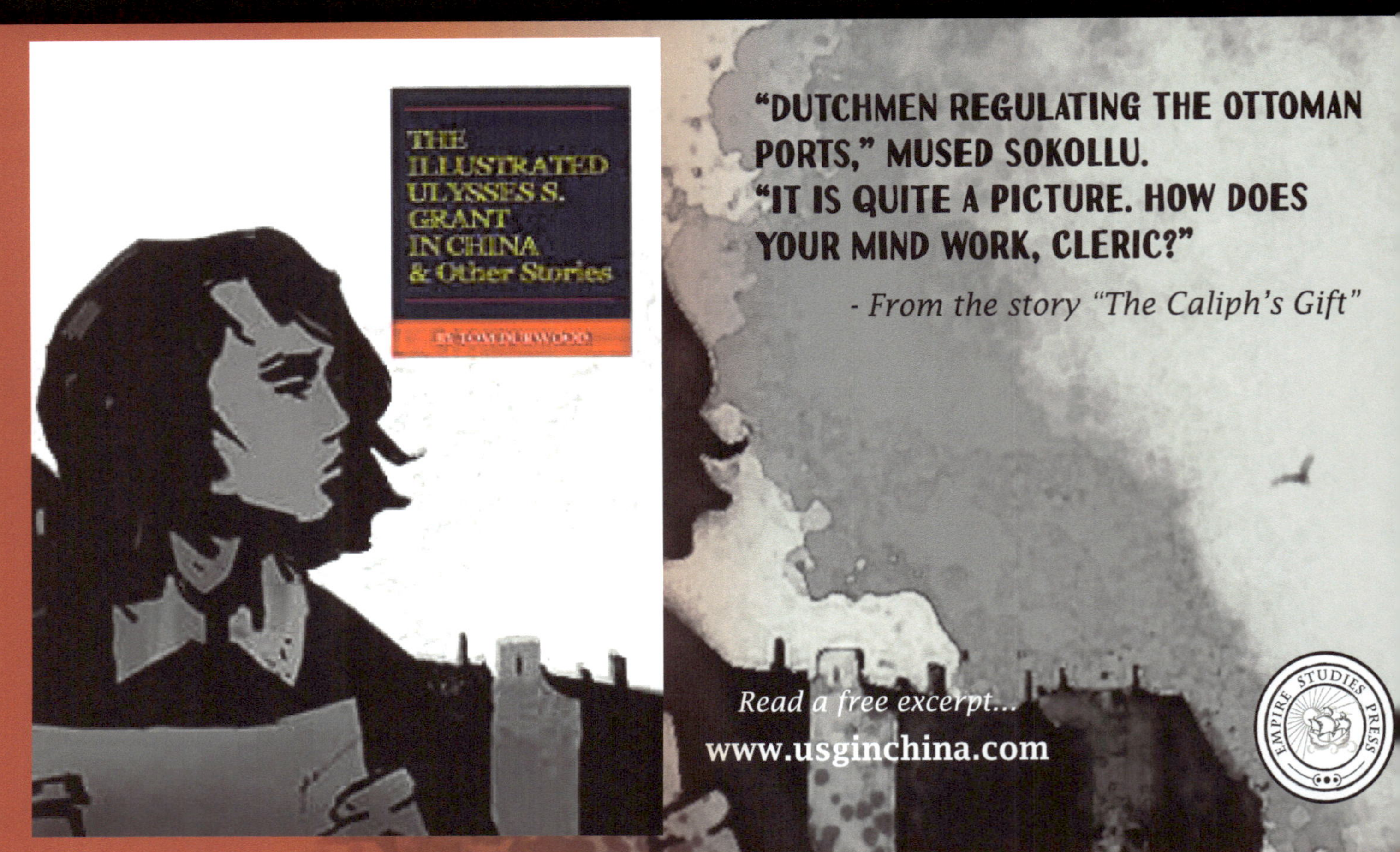

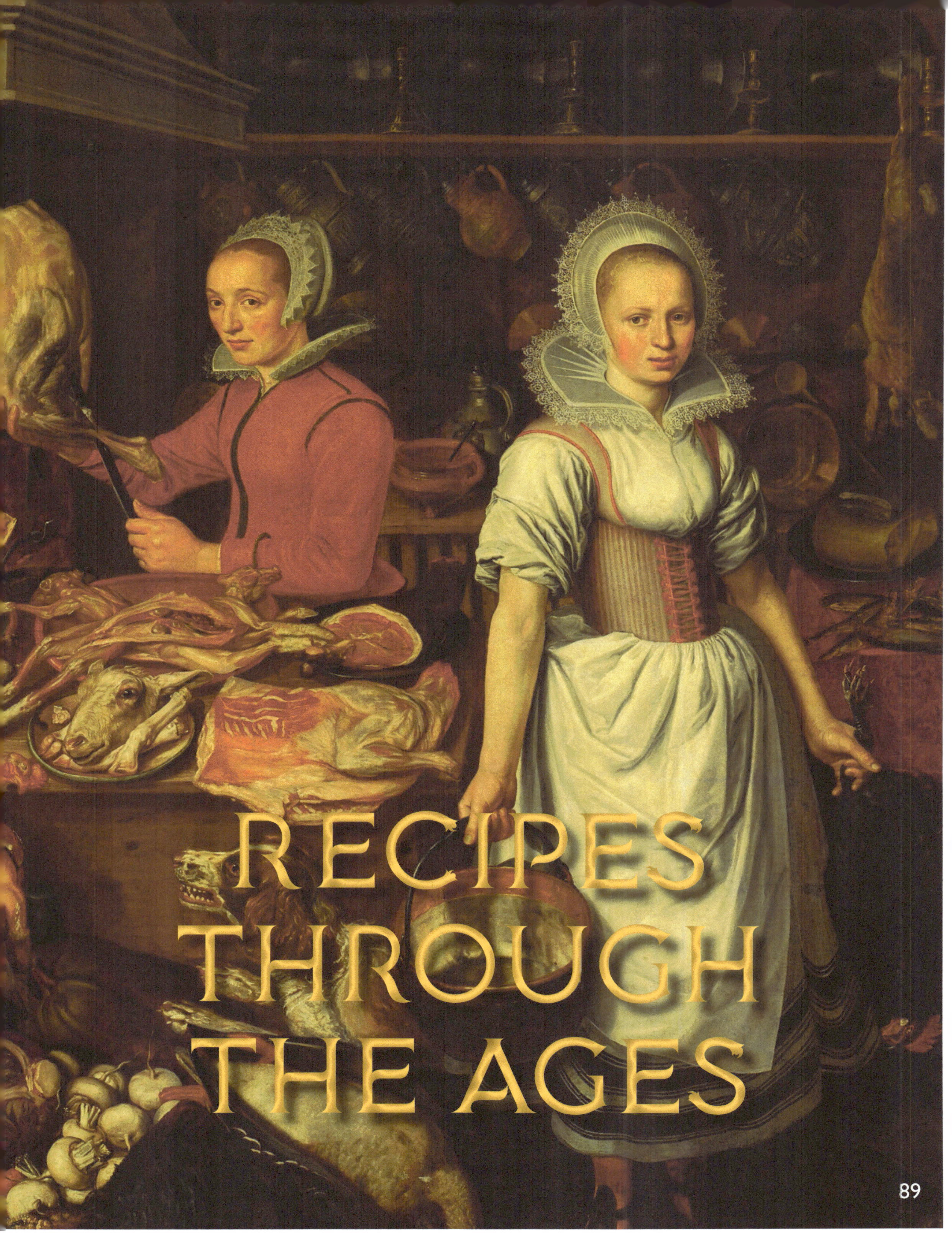

RECIPES THROUGH THE AGES

"I've been making this recipe for years. It is quite simply the best Irish stew recipe I've found and is a hearty meal for a cold winter night. Best served with a crusty bread while reading an immersive Irish historical novel." - Dee Marley

Liam Neeson's Glens of Atrim Stew

1 oz/25 g butter
2 lb/900 g lamb or beef, cubed
1 large onion, coarsely chopped
2 carrots, chopped
1 tbsp plain flour (optional)
0.5 pint/275 ml beef stock
2 tbsp tomato puree
0.5 tbsp sugar
2 potatoes, cubed (optional)
1 bottle of Guinness or a large glass of red wine
1 bouquet garni (sprig of parsley, sprig of thyme, 1 bay leaf tied up in muslin)
Salt and freshly ground black pepper
Tabasco sauce

Method:

Melt the butter in a large pan and fry the meat in it until browned on all sides. Do not crowd the pan; brown the meat in two or three batches if necessary. Remove the meat from the pan, add the onion and carrots and cook until slightly softened.
Return the meat to the pan, add the flour, if using, then stir in the stock, tomato puree and sugar. Bring to the boil and then reduce the heat to a simmer. Add the potatoes, if using, the Guinness or the wine, the bouquet garni and salt and pepper to taste.
Cook over a low heat for about 1 to 1 1/2 hours or until the meat is tender. While the stew is simmering, add 4 or 5 drops of tabasco to taste.

"Serve with good bread, a bottle of wine, such as Margaux '85, and Van Morrison's 'Celtic Twilight' playing in the background." --Liam Neeson

Welsh Cakes. (Makes about 12)

2 oz (56g) dripping (traditionally lard, but butter or
baking fat can be used)
6 oz (170g) self raising flour.
¼ teaspoon ground nutmeg.
2 oz (56g) sugar
2 oz (56g) mixed dried fruit (or 1 oz dried fruit and
1 oz fresh grated carrot – a WW2 variation)
1 egg.
1 tablespoon milk

Method:

Rub the fat into the flour.
Add the spice, sugar and dried fruit.
Add egg and milk and mix to a stiff dough.
Roll out into half inch thickness and cut into 3 inch
rounds.
Pre heat and grease ahead a griddle or heavy frying
pan.
Put in the Welsh cakes and cook until Golden
Brown on both sides. (Lovely served hot with but-
ter.)

Bara Brith (Speckled Bread)

400 grammes (14 oz) mixed fruit
300 millilitres (8 fl oz) strong tea.
250 grammes (8 oz) self raising flour
One teaspoon mixed spice
100 grammes (4 oz) dark brown muscovado sugar
1 egg, beaten

Method:

Put the dried fruit in a bowl and pour over the tea. Mix in the sugar and stir well to dissolve. Leave to soak for at least 6 hours or overnight.
Next day, sift the flour and spices into the soaked fruit (no need to drain the tea) and stir in the egg. Blend well together.
Pre heat the oven to 180 °C/350°F/Gas 4.
Line a 900 gramme loaf tin with baking paper and pour in the mixture.
Bake for approximately one hour until the cake has risen and cooked through. Leave to cool on a rack and store for two days before eating. Served sliced with butter.

Cawl* (Lamb and root vegetable soup)

*pronounced to rhyme with howl

600 grammes (1 ¼ lb) lamb (any will do, preferably bone in) seasoned with salt and pepper
Oil
2 large potatoes
2 carrots
2 parsnips
2 turnips
1 swede
2 leeks
Thyme or parsley
To serve bread, butter and a Hank of strong cheese, for example,
Caerphilly or Cheddar

Method:

Sear meat in oil in a large heavy pan till browned on all sides.
Add 2 litres (4 ½ pints) of water to the pan and bring to the boil.
Lower to a simmer and add all root vegetables except the leeks. Simmer uncovered for two to three hours till the meat is so tender it falls apart. Skim any fat that rises if you wish.
Twenty minutes before you're ready to serve, add the leeks to the pan.
When the cawl is ready, take out the meat and shredded town, taking care to discard all the bones (if you've used meat with bones in). Return the meat to the soup. Taste it before you season it.
Finally, sprinkle with fresh thyme or parsley and serve in deep bowls, accompanied by good fresh bread and strong cheese.

Dorset Apple Cake

115 grammes (4 oz) butter
225 grammes (8 oz) self raising flour
2 teaspoons ground cinnamon,
115 grammes (4 oz) light brown sugar
1 large egg
6-8 tablespoons milk
225 grammes (8 oz) Bramley or Granny Smith apples
peeled, cored and diced
100 grammes (3 ½ oz) sultanas
2 tablespoons of demerara sugar optional

Method:

Heat the oven to 180 °C (160 °C Fan)/350°F (310°F)/Gas 4.
Grease and line a deep 20 centimetre cake tin with baking parchment.
Mix the flour and cinnamon together in a large bowl. Add the butter and rub into the flour using your fingers said it resembles fine breadcrumbs.
Stir in the light brown sugar.
Beat in the egg, followed by 6 to 8 tablespoons of milk until you have a smooth, thick better.
Add the apples and sultanas and mix to combine.
Put the batter into the prepared tin and gently level out.
Sprinkle over the demerara sugar if using and bake for 30 to 40 minutes, or until golden and a skewer put into the middle comes out clean.
Allowed to cool in the tin for 15 minutes, and then carefully turn out onto a wire rack to cool further.
Best served warm with a little custard.

Scottish Tablet (a kind of fudge)

4 oz margarine or butter
1 full cup fresh milk (unsweetened)
1 ½ lb granulated sugar
1 tin (can) condensed milk (I assume 14 oz or 397 g)

Method:

Melt margarine in pan, add sugar and fresh milk. Stir well. Bring to boiling point and cook rapidly for 5 minutes.
Add tin of condensed milk and bring to boil again for 5 minutes. (Stir well and continue cooking till mixture changes colour and starts to thicken.
Remove from heat and beat again for 2 to 3 minutes.
Pour into a lined swiss roll tin and leave to cool. Cut into squares.

Kedgeree (for 4)

"This is my mother's version of a British dish based on Indian food experienced in India – popular from Victorian times as a breakfast dish). This is the version I was taught to cook, although I now spice it up a lot more and sometimes use mackerel or salmon instead and we've always eaten it for brunch or dinner. I'm guessing at the quantities as I just do it from memory and tend to adapt with what I have. My mother's recipe is not from Victorian times but the recipe is still popular!" - historical author, Paula Harmon

250g haddock (dyed or undyed)
100 ml fresh milk
200g basmati rice
4 tomatoes sliced
4 hard-boiled eggs - halved
½ teaspoon turmeric powder
½ teaspoon cayenne powder
Butter

Method:

Cook the rice according to instructions with the turmeric. Drain.
Meanwhile poach the haddock in the milk until it is flaking, adding cayenne towards the end.
Pre-heat a grill (broiler) and butter an oven proof dish.
Mix the drained rice, fish and milk together and put into the oven proof dish. Put the halved eggs and sliced tomatoes on top, dot with butter and put under the grill (broiler) for a short time.
Serve.

(Variations – nowadays I'd cook the rice and meanwhile saute an onion, add some curry paste, add smoked mackerel or salmon and stir till warmed through, then add the cooked rice and some cooked peas and sliced tomatoes and serve from the pan with the halved boiled eggs on the side.)

Bad Mummy Cheese Scones

8oz (250g) self-raising flour
2oz (50g) soft spread or butter
4oz (125g) grated strong cheddar
1oz (25g) mustard (dry or made)
3-4ish tablespoons of milk (you may need more or less depending on the flour)

Method:

Put oven on to 200°C (400°F Gas 6) and line a baking tray with greaseproof or oven paper.
While oven is heating up, mix the flour and rub in the spread or butter. If using dry mustard put it in before spread and mix with flour, if using made mustard add it after you rubbed in the spread (if you get it wrong the world will not end but someone might end up with a bit more mustard in their bite)
Mix in almost all the grated cheese.
Mix in the milk, bit by bit until you have a soft ball. If it's a bit wet add some flour, if it's too dry, add some milk.
Divide the dough into six or eight and roll each section into a ball and put onto baking sheet.
Flatten each scone slightly and sprinkle on the remaining grated cheese.
Pop in oven for ten minutes. They are done when the bottom is slightly brown and you can "knock" on them.
Best eaten hot from the oven with butter.

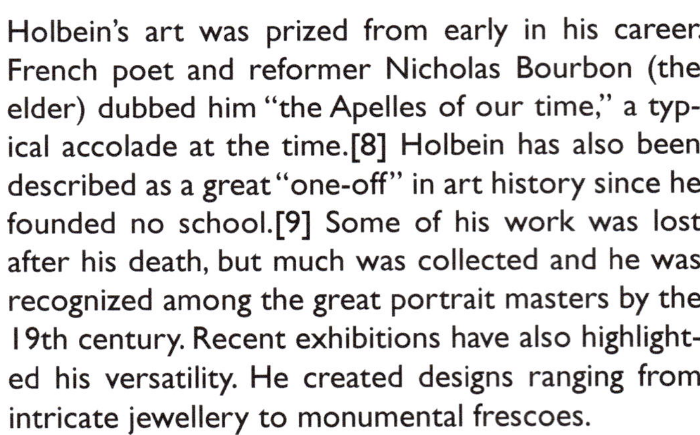

HANS HOLBEIN the Younger
(1497 - 1593)

Holbein was born in Augsburg but worked mainly in Basel as a young artist. At first, he painted murals and religious works, and designed stained glass windows and illustrations for books from the printer Johann Froben. He also painted an occasional portrait, making his international mark with portraits of humanist Desiderius Erasmus of Rotterdam. When the Reformation reached Basel, Holbein worked for reformist clients while continuing to serve traditional religious patrons. His Late Gothic style was enriched by artistic trends in Italy, France, and the Netherlands, as well as by Renaissance humanism. The result was a combined aesthetic uniquely his own.

Holbein travelled to England in 1526 in search of work with a recommendation from Erasmus. He was welcomed into the humanist circle of Thomas More, where he quickly built a high reputation. He returned to Basel for four years, then resumed his career in England in 1532 under the patronage of Anne Boleyn and Thomas Cromwell. By 1535, he was King's Painter to Henry VIII of England. In this role, he produced portraits and festive decorations, as well as designs for jewellery, plate, and other precious objects. His portraits of the royal family and nobles are a record of the court in the years when Henry was asserting his supremacy over the Church of England.

Holbein's art was prized from early in his career. French poet and reformer Nicholas Bourbon (the elder) dubbed him "the Apelles of our time," a typical accolade at the time.[8] Holbein has also been described as a great "one-off" in art history since he founded no school.[9] Some of his work was lost after his death, but much was collected and he was recognized among the great portrait masters by the 19th century. Recent exhibitions have also highlighted his versatility. He created designs ranging from intricate jewellery to monumental frescoes.

Holbein's art has sometimes been called realist, since he drew and painted with a rare precision. His portraits were renowned in their time for their likeness, and it is through his eyes that many famous figures of his day are pictured today, such as Erasmus and More. He was never content with outward appearance, however; he embedded layers of symbolism, allusion, and paradox in his art, to the lasting fascination of scholars. In the view of art historian Ellis Waterhouse, his portraiture "remains unsurpassed for sureness and economy of statement, penetration into character, and a combined richness and purity of style".

IOANNES HOLPENIVS BA   SILEENSIS
SVI IPSIVS EFFIGIATOR   Æ XLV
ETATIS   SVÆ XLIX

Holbein returned to England, where the political and religious environment was changing radically. In 1532, Henry VIII was preparing to repudiate Catherine of Aragon and marry Anne Boleyn, in defiance of the pope. Among those who opposed Henry's actions was Holbein's former host and patron Sir Thomas More, who resigned as Lord Chancellor in May 1532. Around this time, Holbein is supposed to have decorated the mortuary roll of John Islip, abbot of Westminster, one of the last mortuary rolls created. Holbein seems to have distanced himself from More's humanist milieu on this visit, and "he deceived those to whom he was recommended", according to Erasmus.[75] The artist found favour instead within the radical new power circles of the Boleyn family and Thomas Cromwell. Cromwell became the king's secretary in 1534, controlling all aspects of government, including artistic propaganda. More was executed in 1535 along with John Fisher, whose portrait Holbein had also drawn.

Holbein's commissions in the early stages of his second English period included portraits of Lutheran merchants of the Hanseatic League. The merchants lived and plied their trade at the Steelyard, a complex of warehouses, offices, and dwellings on the north bank of the Thames. Holbein rented a house in Maiden Lane nearby, and he portrayed his clients in a range of styles. His portrait of Georg Giese of Gdańsk shows the merchant surrounded by exquisitely painted symbols of his trade. His portrait of Derich Berck of Cologne, on the other hand, is classically simple and possibly influenced by Titian.[78] For the guildhall of the Steelyard, Holbein painted the monumental allegories The Triumph of Wealth and The Triumph of Poverty, both now lost. The merchants also commissioned a street tableau of Mount Parnassus for Anne Boleyn's coronation eve procession of 31 May 1533.

Holbein also portrayed various courtiers, landowners, and visitors during this time, and his most famous painting of the period was The Ambassadors. This life-sized panel portrays Jean de Dinteville, an ambassador of Francis I of France in 1533, and Georges de Selve, Bishop of Lavaur who visited London the same year. The work incorporates symbols and paradoxes, including an anamorphic (distorted) skull. According to scholars, these are enigmatic references to learning, religion, mortality, and illusion in the tradition of the Northern Renaissance. Art historians Oskar Bätschmann and Pascal Griener suggest that in The Ambassadors, "Sciences and arts, objects of luxury and glory, are measured against the grandeur of Death".

No certain portraits survive of Anne Boleyn by Holbein, perhaps because her memory was purged following her execution for treason, incest, and adultery in 1536. It is clear, however, that Holbein worked directly for Anne and her circle. He designed a cup engraved with her device of a falcon standing on roses, as well as jewellery and books connected to her. He also sketched several women attached to her entourage, including her sister-in-law Jane Parker. At the same time, Holbein worked for Thomas Cromwell as he masterminded Henry VIII's reformation. Cromwell commissioned Holbein to produce reformist and royalist images, including anti-clerical woodcuts and the title page to Myles Coverdale's English translation of the Bible. Henry VIII had embarked on a grandiose programme of artistic patronage. His efforts to glorify his new status as Supreme Head of the Church culminated in the building of Nonsuch Palace, which started in 1538.

By 1536, Holbein was employed as the King's Painter on an annual salary of 30 pounds—though he was never the highest-paid artist on the royal payroll. Royal "pictor maker" Lucas Horenbout earned more, and other continental artists also worked for the king. In 1537, Holbein painted his most famous image: Henry VIII standing in a heroic pose with his feet planted apart. The left section has survived of Holbein's cartoon for a life-sized wall painting at Whitehall Palace showing the king in this pose with his father behind him. The mural also depicted Jane Seymour and Elizabeth of York, but it was destroyed by fire in 1698. It is known from engravings and from a 1667 copy by Remigius van Leemput. An earlier half-length portrait shows Henry in a similar pose, but all the full-length portraits of him are copies based on the Whitehall pattern. The figure of Jane Seymour in the mural is related to Holbein's sketch and painting of her.
Jane died in October 1537, shortly after bearing Henry's only legitimate son Edward VI, and Holbein painted a portrait of the infant prince about two years later, clutching a sceptre-like gold rattle. Holbein's final portrait of Henry dates from 1543 and was perhaps completed by others, depicting the king with a group of barber surgeons.

Holbein's portrait style altered after he entered Henry's service. He focused more intensely on the sitter's face and clothing, largely omitting props and three-dimensional settings. He applied this clean, craftsman-like technique to miniature portraits such as that of Jane Small, and to grand portraits such as that of Christina of Denmark. He travelled with Philip Hoby to Brussels in 1538 and sketched Christina for the king, who was appraising the young widow as a prospective bride. John Hutton, the English ambassador in Brussels, reported that another artist's drawing of Christina was "sloberid" (slobbered) compared to Holbein's.

In Wilson's view, Holbein's subsequent oil portrait is "the loveliest painting of a woman that he ever executed, which is to say that it is one of the finest female portraits ever painted". The same year, Holbein and Hoby went to France to paint Louise of Guise and Anna of Lorraine for Henry VIII. Neither portrait of these cousins has survived. Holbein found time to visit Basel, where he was fêted by the authorities and granted a pension. On the way back to England, he apprenticed his son Philipp to Basel-born goldsmith Jacob David in Paris.

Holbein painted Anne of Cleves at Burgau Castle, posing her square-on and in elaborate finery. This was the woman whom Henry married at Düren at the encouragement of Thomas Cromwell in the summer of 1539. English envoy Nicholas Wotton reported that "Hans Holbein hath taken the effigies of my Lady Anne and the lady Amelia [Anne's sister] and hath expressed their images very lively". Henry was disillusioned with Anne in the flesh, however, and he divorced her after a brief, unconsummated marriage. There is a tradition that Holbein's portrait flattered Anne, derived from the testimony of Sir Anthony Browne.

Henry said that he was dismayed by her appearance at Rochester, having seen her pictures and heard advertisements of her beauty—so much that his face fell. No one other than Henry ever described Anne as repugnant; French Ambassador Charles de Marillac thought her quite attractive, pleasant, and dignified, though dressed in unflattering, heavy German clothing, as were her attendants. Some of the blame for the king's disillusionment fell on Thomas Cromwell, who had been instrumental in arranging the marriage and had passed on some exaggerated claims of Anne's beauty. This was one of the factors that led to Cromwell's downfall.

Sources and Images from Wikipedia.

WINNING HISTORY

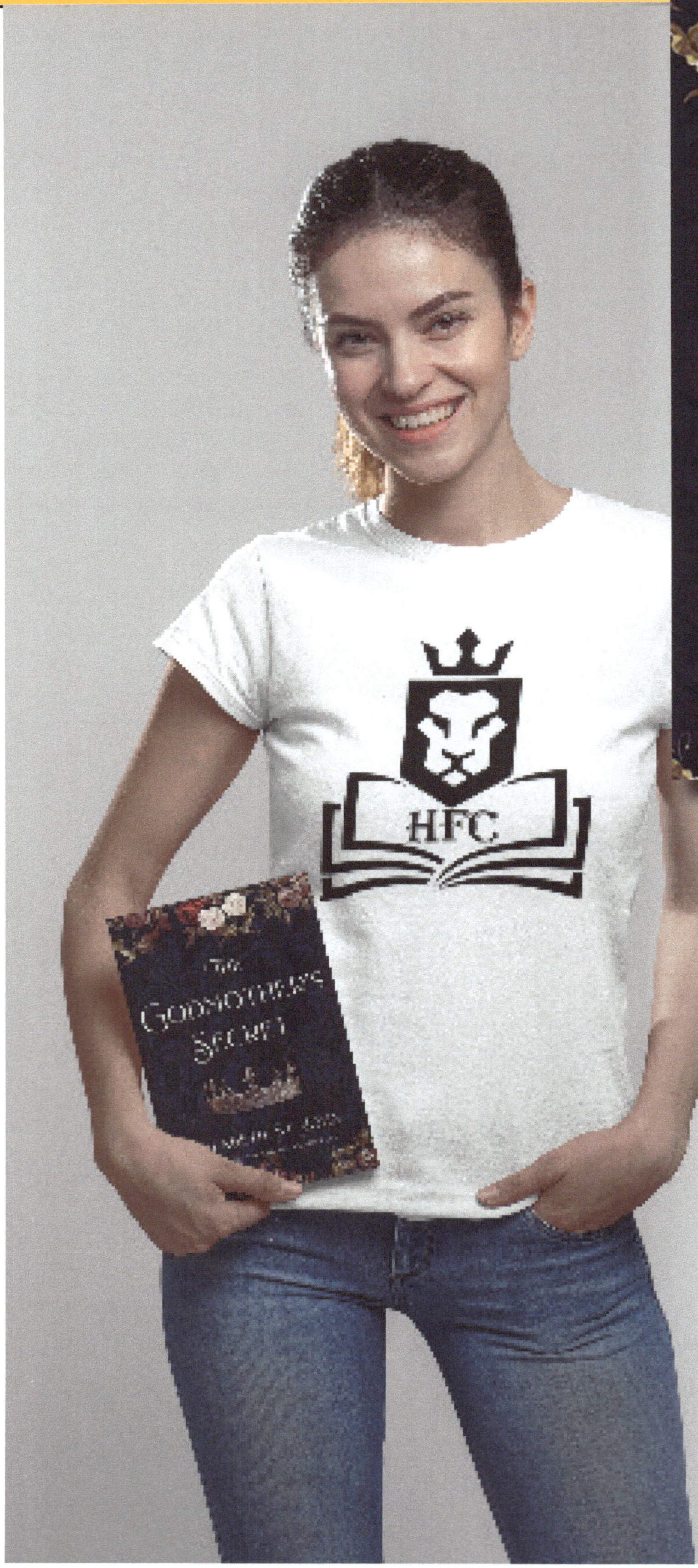

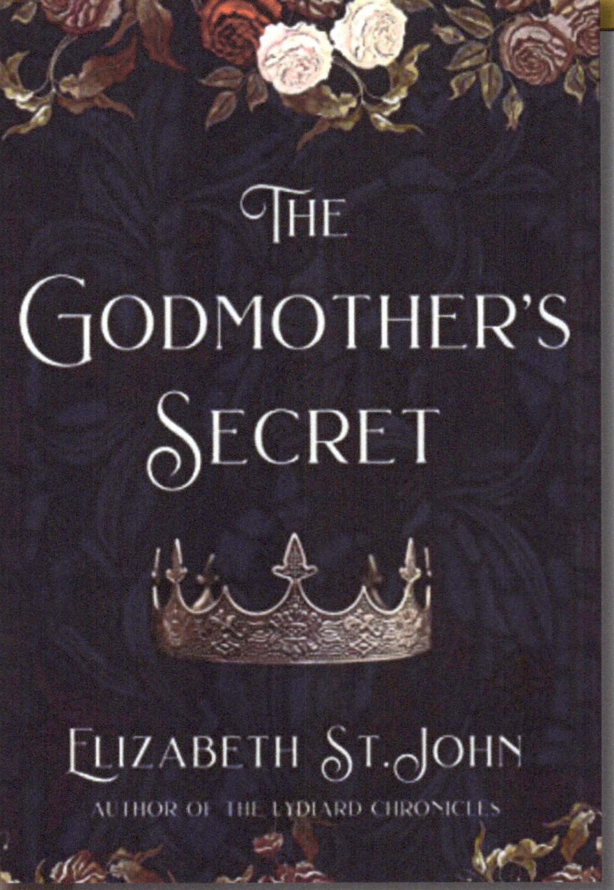

ENTER TO WIN:
A signed copy of
"The Godmother's Secret"
by Elizabeth St. John,
plus a HFC t-shirt!

You must fill out crossword, take a picture of your entry and email to thehistoricalfictioncompany@gmail.com along with your shirt size.

Great Britain, Scotland, Ireland

Down:

1. the middle name of the man who shot Lincoln
3. the last name of the first woman diarist in the late 17th-century
5. a Scottish dish with pig innards
7. Who is the Duke of Rothesay and Lord of the Isles today?
9. the red rose house in the War of the Roses
11. the city setting for Ella Carey's new book
12. the ship taken by Fletcher Christian in the famous mutiny
13. an island in the Saint Kilda archipelago
14. the last name of a king which is also an era in English history

Across:

2. last name of the man who painted Henry VIII's famous portrait
4. the NASA space center is in this city in Texas
6. the concentration camp liberated in April of 1945
8. the name of Lord Nelson and Emma Hamilton's child
10. a baked good delicious with clotted cream and cream tea
11. the blighted vegetable in Ireland in the 1800s
12. the field where Richard III died
15. the last name of the 'middling' family who wrote a lot of letters during the WOTR
16. the name of the street for the 1974 IRA bombings

The Historical Fiction Company

HFC Book of the Year Awards
$1000 Cash Prize plus Book Marketing

Quality Editorial Reviews

Custom Book Cover
& Book Trailer Design

Online Bookshop & Author Profiles

NEW! History Podcast
featuring author interviews & history content episodes

www.thehistoricalfictioncompany.com

The   Book of
Coffee Pot   the Year
Book Club   Awards

The Coffee Pot Book Club

The Coffee Pot Book Club was founded in 2015 as a platform that would help authors of Historical Fiction (and its sub-genres, such as Historical Romance, Fantasy, Mystery, or Time Travel / Dual-Timeline) promote their books and find that sometimes elusive audience. Since then, The Coffee Pot Book Club has become a trusted place for readers to meet new authors (both traditionally and independently published) and discover their fabulous books.

PROMOTING QUALITY HISTORICAL FICTION SINCE 2015

https://thecoffeepotbookclub.blogspot.com/

Historium Press Classics
Jane Austen Collection

Now available on Amazon
or The Historical Fiction Company bookshop,
with forewords by award-winning Regency authors!

THE BOOK OF URIEL by Elyse Hoffman

"An otherworldly tale with indelible characters in a realistic wartime setting. Hoffman's novel sublimely fuses world history and Jewish folklore."—Kirkus Reviews

The Douglas Bastard
J. R. TOMLIN

Young Archibald, the Black Douglas's bastard son, returns from exile to a Scotland ravaged by war. The war-hardened Knight of Liddesdale will teach him what he must learn. And with danger on every side, he must learn to sleep with one eye open and a claymore in his hand because even their closest ally may betray them...

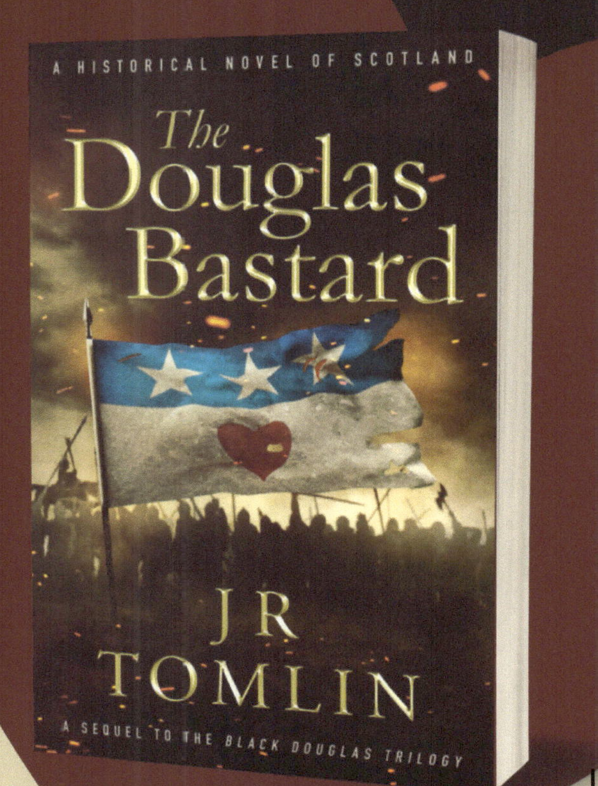

NOW AT AMAZON

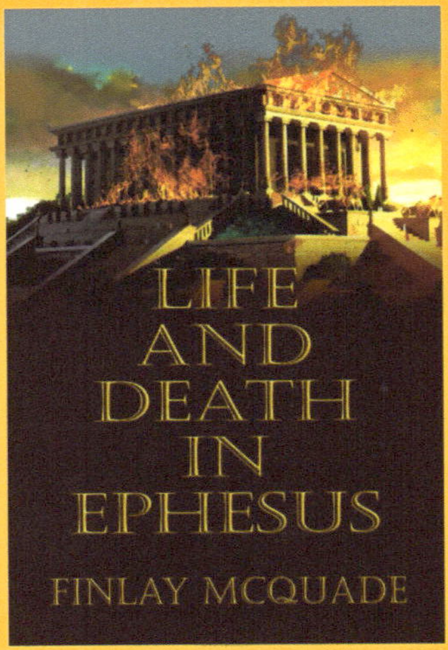

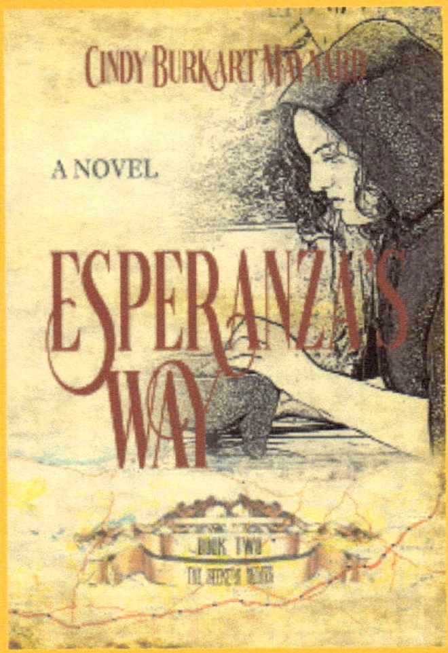